WHITE HAT BLACK HEART

CYBER TEEN PROJECT BOOK 1

D. B. GOODIN

Cover design by Andrew Dobell.

Editing by Wandering Words Media

Proofread by Wandering Words Media

For more information about the Cyber Teen Project series visit:

https://www.davidgoodinauthor.com.

ISBN: 978-1-7334202-1-1 (Paperback)

ISBN: 978-1-7334202-0-4 (e-book)

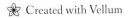

❀ Created with Vellum

For my Family

PREFACE

I have altered the names of specific technology used in this book to protect copyrights. I got the idea for this book back in 2011, when I noticed an upward trend in data breaches. I had only been in the security space a few years and was just starting a Master's program in Digital Forensics. One goal for this book is to teach young people basic Cybersecurity concepts in a fun and engaging fashion. There is a shortage of qualified Cybersecurity professionals, and if this book piques the interest of young people, then the book has met its goal.

CHAPTER 1

THE SUN SHONE on Nigel Watson's face as he picked up the remaining pieces of trash. Of all the volunteer service activities, Nigel enjoyed the beach cleanup days the most. The sounds of the waves crashing on the shore and the heat of the sun relaxed him. Nigel gazed out over a jewel-like ocean to enjoy another spectacular view before he returned to the beach parking lot to drop off collected trash, equipment, get his log signed, and go home. Just as Nigel was contemplating this, Milo appeared from behind a sand dune.

"Hey, Nige! Any weekend plans?"

"Not much; going to play *The Machine*, I think."

The Colossal Machine was an online role-playing game that had been taking up most of his weekends lately.

"I might do that, although my dad did just get me a cool new antenna kit to construct. Either way, we should hang out. We haven't since summer."

They began walking toward the parking lot together, the sun bearing down on them.

"We'll see how it goes. I need to develop some characters for Jake and his friend."

"I don't know why you do that. I know it's extra money, but you have been missing a lot of school lately."

"I haven't been feeling well," Nigel lied.

They dropped off their equipment. Nigel's mother's black Ford sedan caught his eye, and he waved.

"Well, call me if you change your mind, Nige."

Milo was already in line to get his service log signed. As Nigel got in line behind him, he heard his phone chirp. It was Jake. Nigel swallowed hard.

"Give me the account."

Nigel typed one word, "Tuesday!"

"Deliver or ur ass is mine."

Nigel swore under his breath. He wanted to get on Jake's good side—if he had one—because the cash was too good to pass up. Nigel looked up from his phone; a dozen or so kids were in front of Milo, and the line wasn't moving fast. At the rate of speed Nigel had been going on the design, it would take the rest of the long weekend to finish Jake's character.

But what if he used the game's macro and programming features normally reserved for modifications to level Jake's character?

"See you Tuesday," Nigel told Milo. "Got to get to work. I'll get this log signed after school instead." As Nigel approached his mother's car, he noticed her going through a stack of papers. His mother was working Saturdays and bringing work home again. She worked too hard. At the beginning, it was great without her around to nag him, but lately having to make his own lunch and look after this younger brother Ralphie wasn't worth the hassle.

"Hi, Mom. Did you have a good day at work?"

His mother Ellen Watson looked up. "Yes, Sweetie. I'm glad I'm off."

Nigel was already in another world: the mobile app version of the game he was addicted to, Pretzelverse's *The Colossal Machine.*

"How was your beach cleanup day?" Ellen continued when he didn't respond.

"It was good."

"Did you get your service log signed?"

"The line was long, so I'll do it Monday."

"Nigel, you forgot to get your log signed last time and missed out on ten hours of community service. Did you forget Monday's a school holiday?" Ellen chided. "This will affect your rating in the honors society."

"I'll get it signed, Mom," Nigel snapped.

"Yes, you will." She whipped the car around. "Today!"

Nigel threw his head back and groaned.

When Ellen arrived at the beach, the event was already packed up, and there was no one to be found. Ellen grumbled as she pulled out of the parking lot and headed toward the district office.

"You always do this, Nigel."

"What? I will get it done at school, Mom; let's just go home," Nigel pleaded.

"You would almost be home if you waited in line like you're supposed to. Why are you so lazy?"

Nigel folded his arms and looked out the window. Ten minutes later, she pulled up to the office. The windows were shuttered. Nigel didn't immediately make a move to go inside; he was still on his phone.

Ellen gave him a gentle push. "We're going to be late to pick up your brother," she said. "Go."

Nigel mumbled something unintelligible as he left the car and slowly moved toward the door.

The community service supervisor sat at a desk going through papers. Helping him was a girl Nigel had never seen before. She was six feet tall, skinny, and had the most captivating smile. Pink streaks ran throughout her golden blonde hair.

"Can I get this log signed?" Nigel asked.

The girl took it from Nigel. After a brief glance, she handed the log back to Nigel.

"I need you to fill this out completely. If you don't, you won't get credit."

Nigel stared back with a blank expression.

"You're missing the correct date of service," the girl said.

Nigel smiled at the girl as he took back the paper. Their hands briefly touched, sending shivers down Nigel's neck. He quickly added the correct information. He wanted to ask her name, but when he opened his mouth and started to speak, he froze. She was gone. Only the community supervisor remained. Nigel gave the log to the supervisor; she signed it and gave it back without so much as a second glance.

"What was the name of the girl who was helping me?" Nigel asked.

"Josephine, but she goes by Jet."

"I like her hair, very captivating."

"Yeah, but the pink streaks are too much."

"Thank you."

He left with a strange feeling in his gut.

Other than a couple side conversations with Milo, Nigel's weekend was spent on the computer, leveling up Jake's character to level thirty-five (out of a possible seventy). Nigel was investing as many hours as another would doing a part-time job.

He navigated Jake's character through the virtual world of *The Colossal Machine*, realizing a more efficient leveling process was needed, then froze as a single thought entered his mind: *I forgot to work on my class project.*

Nigel sighed. *Sleep will have to wait. Where are those machine learning project notes?* He didn't want to be caught without any progress, especially since this was the only class Nigel liked.

Nigel needed a way to continue leveling up Jake's character in the background while working on his project. Pretzelverse, the game developer, allowed users to make enhancements to the game without modifying its core code. After a few searches, Nigel found an article by a programmer who removed much of the graphical interface, allowing the game to run on less powerful computers. A link to a demonstration video was embedded into the article. Nigel watched in amazement as a scene of a forest transformed into text-based characters. He noticed a tree having several rotated equal signs for the trunk and greater- and less-than symbols for the leaves. While this approach wasn't perfect, it did a decent job of showing the world without real graphics. The modification was so good that Pretzelverse awarded the Modder its best game modification award at its annual gamer conference in Cologne, Germany.

Nigel thought he could use this information to virtualize a subset of his operating system and accommodate running the game in the background without taking too much of his computer's resources.

Before long, Nigel found the original modification programmer, or Modder, had a page on Prog-hub, a site most programmers used to share their work. His project was called PretUIModder. Nigel downloaded the program, and in a few short hours he was leveling Jake's character while simultaneously writing code for his class project. Nigel worked until his eyes began to ache. He drifted off to sleep.

Nigel woke up on Tuesday feeling like his brain was in a fog. He knew he spent way too much time playing the game for his classmates this weekend—nearly sixty hours in total.

Usually he took Saturday off but got talked into accepting two last-minute paying customers on Friday afternoon. Jake practically forced his way in. Nigel reluctantly agreed because Jake and his friend were paying $150 each.

They even paid in advance!

Nigel rubbed his eyes in exhaustion. He had underestimated the amount of time it would take to level the characters to max level. Over the weekend, he only managed to gain another five levels. *Argh, this is taking forever.*

Ellen awoke to an annoying buzzing sound that she could not place.

What day is it?

She had worked a double shift at the telemarketers' union because her co-worker, Linda, called in sick. Time seemed to blend together with her excessively late working schedule. The telemarketers' union specialized in solving problems or conflicts with members' work assignments. Ellen's work was very routine; however, sometimes clients were belligerent, verbally abusive, or difficult. She could transfer them to another level up the chain, but lost points if she did it too often. Yesterday she had encountered plenty of belligerence, but lost zero points, which was a benefit to her paycheck (and a detriment to her mental health).

When she finally opened her eyes, the clock read 7:45!

"Holy crap! I'm going to be late!"

Ellen needed to hurry this morning, but she had her boys to consider, and she wanted to make sure that they got a good breakfast. She knew Nigel skipped a number of meals due to his computer game addiction. Ellen didn't care for the constant late nights. She planned to address the problem on Saturday, her only day off this week. *He's going to spend some time with me no matter what*, Ellen thought bitterly.

Ellen knocked on Nigel's door. When he didn't reply, she opened the door and found Nigel playing video games.

"This is the last time," Ellen said.

"What?"

"I don't know why I try so hard to get you to be responsible when all you want to do is play childish games," Ellen demanded.

Nigel said nothing.

"You are a solid B student. I know you can bring at least one of those grades to an A. You are more than capable of entering a good engineering school, but with your track record, you're going to be lucky to get into community college!" Ellen wondered if Nigel even cared about getting into college at all. "You have ten minutes, then I'm leaving." Ellen slammed the door.

Nigel's plan for work was simple: develop a game-leveling business and do the odd hacking or coding on the side. He didn't need to spend four years at a college when he could make money with his current business. He didn't need a degree at all.

According to Nigel, there were two things that prospective employers wanted: good coding skills and a good work ethic. In addition to his homework, Nigel was putting twelve-plus hours a day into his business, which he had carefully developed and nurtured from nothing. He was creating online characters for popular games and reselling them for a profit (at least most of the time). The last thing he needed was college.

CHAPTER 2

Nigel could access the computer lab anytime school was open, even between school periods. Aside from Mr. Levinson's class, the lab had the best connectivity in the entire school. When Nigel arrived, he had to stop short of running into another student; there was a small but noticeable line to the computer lab.

"What's going on?" Nigel said aloud to no one in particular.

"New reader system," the boy in front of him said. "You have to scan your school ID."

Nigel nodded in acknowledgement. He recognized the boy; he had seen him around when the computer lab just opened. Nigel thought his name was George.

When they finally reached the front of the line, George waved his badge atop the reader and entered. Nigel was about to do the same when he heard a familiar voice.

"Hey, Chum."

To Nigel's horror, it was Jake!

"Got to go to the lab," Nigel said and stepped in.

Jake suddenly cut the line but was stopped by a tall and burly proctor.

"Swipe your badge for entry. No tailgating," the proctor demanded.

Jake tried swiping his school badge. A red light and audible negative tone emitted from the reader.

"You do not have access," the proctor said. "Go to school administration and get it fixed."

"Hey, Bonehead, we're not finished," Jake cried as he was escorted out of the computer lab.

As Nigel entered, he glanced at his watch. 3:11 p.m. The lab was fairly dead for this time of day; he counted about eight students. Nigel sat at his favorite terminal at the far side of the lab. It was close to the window, and the desk was big enough for him to work on the desktop and his laptop at the same time. Nigel quickly set up the laptop, did his usual screen obfuscation (which always took several minutes), then finally started working on his project.

Since Mr. Levinson made it clear that he wasn't accepting any computer game projects, Nigel chose machine learning as his backup project. Nigel had heard the buzzword "machine learning" somewhere, but it was so new that most students knew little or nothing about it. It wasn't even in his assigned textbooks yet, and Mr. Levinson almost always used up-to-date materials.

Nigel glanced up from his project long enough to see a girl he recognized. *Oh, the girl from the district office! What was her name?* Nigel frowned in concentration. She tripped and dropped a book just short of Nigel's desk. He quickly got up and retrieved the book and handed it to the girl.

"Thanks," she said.

The cover of the textbook pictured a robot holding a dove in its metal hand. The title read *Electric Dream: The Story of Artificial Intelligence.*

"It's for my project in Mr. Levinson's class," the girl said.

"Cool. My project is on machine learning."

"Awesome," the girl said excitedly. "Most of the kids here are doing something trivial like creating games. You are the first person I met who actually has something worthwhile."

"What is your name?" Nigel asked, swallowing back his urge to argue that there was nothing trivial about creating games.

"Josephine. But all my friends call me Jet."

"I'm Nigel."

"I'm so glad we met, Nigel. We should talk soon so we can compare notes."

Nigel thought he noticed Jet blush, but before he could process this thought, Jet gave Nigel a smile and walked away.

Nigel's little brother, Ralphie, sat in his room staring at the load screen for *Kenny Kart Racing*, his favorite game of all time. He wanted to play with his big brother, but Nigel was always preoccupied with his own games. Most of Nigel's games required reading hundreds of lines of dialogue just to complete a single quest. Ralphie had no interest in that. The difficulty level in these games was off the charts. Ralphie enjoyed simple gaming pleasures, and his favorite was *Kenny Kart Racing*. Nigel used to play the multiplayer version with him, but not since he got sucked into The Machine.

"Ralphie, get ready for school. We are already late!" Ellen said.

Ralphie just continued to play his game.

"Turn it off now!" Ellen screamed.

Ralphie immediately turned his system off. He had never seen his mother this upset.

"I have enough trouble with your brother. If these games are too much of a distraction, I will take them away."

"Sorry, Momma," Ralphie said in a weak voice. Ralphie was already dressed and ready to go, so Ellen didn't have to wait long.

The arguments between Nigel and his mother were almost a daily occurrence, so Ralphie used the yelling time to get ready. He usually had some time to play a round or two of *Kenny Kart* before school. This morning, he had played at least a half dozen by the time Ralphie grabbed his lunch box.

"Get in the car now. We're late," Ellen demanded.

Both boys jumped in without saying a word. Ralphie didn't like it when his mother was upset, especially if it was directed at him. Her high-pitched voice seemed to go up a notch or two if she didn't get immediate results, so Ralphie usually listened the first time.

Nigel sat in the back of Mr. Levinson's class, as usual, and connected to the creative thinking private network. Nigel had to be quick, before Mr. Levinson arrived. Wi-Fi access in the classroom was a bit spotty. Nigel thought it had something to do with the wire mesh that covered the walls and ceiling of Mr. Levinson's class.

As other students started entering, Nigel noticed Jet; she waved at him as she sat a row up and a couple seats to the left. It was rare for a girl like Jet to like hacking. He thought her AI idea was one of the most innovative projects in the class. Nigel's eyes drifted back to the computer screen. He launched the text-replacer program modification and minimized its window so no one would notice. He was determined to level Jake's character while in Mr. Levinson's class. *Risky move,* he thought, but the stakes were already high with Jake. He started sweating just thinking about it.

Just as the last student arrived, Mr. Levinson entered the room with a cup of coffee.

"Sorry I'm late, class," Mr. Levinson said as he began closing the door with his free hand. "Screens down."

The sound of laptops clicking closed could be heard throughout the classroom. Unfortunately, Nigel's reaction time was a bit slow. He was in the middle of setting up several controls to help mask his movements so Mr. Levinson wouldn't notice his network activity during class. Mr. Levinson was staring at him, the only student who hadn't closed the lid of his laptop. Out of the corner of his eye, Nigel noticed Jet silently mouthing the word "DOWN."

Seconds later, he shut his laptop.

"Well then," Mr. Levinson said. "Now that Mr. Watson has finally decided to obey class rules, I think he should start our daily show-and-tell session. What do you think, class?" Mr. Levinson didn't wait for a response before he continued. "Mr. Watson, you have fifteen minutes to convince me not to throw you out of my class."

Nigel's mouth ran dry; his hands were trembling slightly.

"NOW," Mr. Levinson barked.

Nigel slowly gathered his laptop and charger.

"I have no available outlets here, Mr. Watson. I trust that your battery will last for at least fifteen minutes."

Nigel thought he saw a slight grin on his face as he approached the front of the classroom. Nigel felt flushed, his heart raced, and he was starting to sweat. He was not prepared to show the class his project.

The game was still running the screen session in the background. If the program got interrupted now, then Jake's character would probably die, and he would lose whatever he had in his game inventory. If he didn't resurrect his character within ten minutes, all of that character's worldly possessions would spill all over the dead avatar in the game world. Nigel worked too hard to let this happen; he needed to log out of the game gracefully.

Before connecting his laptop to the class projector, he quickly pressed a series of keys. Two Dire Wolves had decided to make a meal of one of Jake's character's legs. Normally, Dire Wolves had only a few dozen hit points and could be dispatched with a few whacks of a sword, but Jake's character was badly injured. Nigel had only one or two moves before the wolves would kill and eat their prey. He decided to move decisively. With a few keystrokes, he was able to summon an apocalypse spell that killed both wolves instantly; however, that meant certain denizens of the dark plane were made aware of these actions. The calculated risk of killing an imminent threat brought consequences. Nigel would need to deal with those consequences later, as there was another more imminent threat to worry about.

Nigel was glad he was in the habit of taking notes in his favorite presentation program. He hoped he would look more prepared than he felt. He opened the presentation program and sent the output to the projector. The words "Project Chaturanga" appeared.

Nigel began talking about the inspiration for the project and why it was an important research project. He briefly discussed the history of Deep Blue, one of the first computers to beat Chess Champion Garry Kasparov. This was one of the first practical uses of artificial intelligence in modern computing. Nigel scanned the room for signs of interest. He noticed that Jet was fixated on his presentation, hanging on every word. Mr. Levinson also looked intrigued.

"The aim of the project is to apply modern machine learning concepts to the game of chess," Nigel continued. "Machine learning makes it possible for technology like artificial intelligence to exist. Think of machine learning as the fuel that drives artificial intelligence. The goal is to have the computer use machine learning to try to figure out what a human might do."

Nigel closed with, "Thank you for your time, class."

At the beginning of the presentation, Nigel was bordering on panic, but now he felt elated.

"We can't wait to see your working prototype two Fridays from now, Mr. Watson," Mr. Levinson said.

Nigel didn't dare reopen his laptop until he was safely away from Mr. Levinson's class. He dreaded logging back in to Jake's account; he had no idea what he was going to find. He had made a bold move casting that spell. When Nigel leveled up a character for a client, he always tried to have an exit strategy for when things in the game got dicey. For Jake, that spell scroll was a lifesaver—and a risky one, at that.

"Hey, Bonehead!" Jake bellowed the moment Nigel left Mr. Levinson's. "Where's my stuff? I want to access my account already!"

Nigel had temporarily changed Jake's password so he would experience minimal interference when power-leveling Jake.

"It's taking a little longer than expected," Nigel said.

"Well, I better have access by the end of the day, or else."

Six Hours Later

Nigel's cell phone rang, and he immediately recognized the number.

"Needlenose!" cried Jake. "Your head is about to meet my fist!"

"What's the matter?" Nigel squeaked.

"My account has been frozen. I just got an email about it! If you don't get my account unlocked or provide a new one by tomorrow, you're in big trouble!" Jake hung up.

Nigel checked his messages; there was an email forwarded from Jake.

CHAPTER 3

NIGEL STARTED to sweat as he read the message.

Greetings Jacob,

We regret to inform you that your account has been put under a temporary suspension pending an investigation. Our anti-fraud system has detected the use of more than one account with an identical source Internet Protocol (IP) address. As a precaution, we have deactivated both accounts in question. If you can prove that the other account is yours, then both accounts will be restored once proof has been submitted. However, it may take three to five business days to verify and to completely restore your account. Please provide two of the following forms of identification to prove your identity.

- Driver's license
- Utility bill
- Credit card statement
- Mortgage bill

Once proof is provided, our customer support staff may need additional verifiable information.

Regards,
Your Friends at Pretzelverse Games

Nigel felt like he had a bowling ball in his throat. The account wasn't hacked; Nigel was caught logging in to more than one account from the same IP address. Although this was not good news, it was far from devastating. At least he had a chance to set things right. Jake was eighteen but might as well be a minor; proving his identity was going to be a bit tricky. Nigel had to think of a good way to convince the customer service people at Pretzelverse to unlock the account.

He immediately called Jake.

"Hello?" Jake answered.

"Hi, Jake."

"Is my account unlocked?"

"I just wanted to say how sorry I am to delay your—"

"I want a discount for this," Jake cut him off. "I'm thinking that free is a fair price. You owe me $150 plus subscription costs. Otherwise, I'm going to be taking that out of your ass."

Nigel was speechless. He had spent the better part of two weeks working on Jake's account. Plus, he already spent the money; there was no way he could recover from that.

"I want my account and the money by the end of tomorrow or there will be hell to pay." Jake hung up.

"Wait!"

Nigel had to ask him if he had a valid driver's license. He called Jake again. After a few rings, he heard an audible *click* and silence. After another few attempts, he was greeted with a prerecorded message, "Your caller is blocking all calls from your number."

Nigel threw his phone across the room. It hit his corkboard at the far end of the room, then fell to the floor with an audible thump.

Nigel would make Jake listen to reason. He needed a copy of his driver's license. He grabbed his bike and started pedaling north down Sycamore Lane.

Nigel had to squint as he rode into the sunset. When Nigel arrived on Front Street, where he thought Jake lived, he shivered as a cold autumn breeze blew across his neck.

Just a few weeks ago, Jake said he wanted a big brute of a character that would wield a big axe and cast spells as fast as a wizard.

"You can't have a character like that."

"Why the hell not?"

"The game doesn't work that way. There are limitations and balance issues to consider," Nigel reasoned.

The game was not limited to predetermined profiles (or classes). Points were awarded for completing quests in the game, or by interacting with the world, other players, and objects. Most games relied on experience points from killing things, but *The Colossal Machine* also rewarded players by doing something that contributed to the world in general. For example, if a character saved another from falling off a cliff or helped another character slay a monster, points would be awarded depending on the difficulty of the task.

Another monitoring system was in place to help combat cheating. If the system detected a large number of repetitive tasks, Game Player Managers (or G.P.M.s) would be summoned to investigate. Other automated systems detected suspicious activity, such as logging on from different IP addresses within a short period of time.

Most of the game's security measures were not public knowledge, but that didn't stop rumor and fan sites from deconstructing everything about the game. Nigel knew these sites well. Pretzelverse was known to fiercely guard their intellectual property, and takedown notices were sent every day to offending fan sites. A large number of these sites wouldn't comply since they were in countries where intellectual property laws didn't exist.

Nigel arrived at Jake's house, confirmed by his mother's battered Dodge Caravan Nigel recognized from school. The original paint job appeared to be maroon, but the car sported several unpainted black sections. Nigel parked his bicycle behind the patchwork that was the Caravan, then proceeded up the steep driveway toward the house.

A strong sense of dread came over Nigel as he rang the doorbell. As soon as he pressed the button, he immediately regretted it. He felt like running back to the safety of his bicycle. He noticed movement out of the corner of his eye. A dirty-looking curtain was being pulled aside, then was quickly closed. A few moments later, the door swung open and a rather formidable-looking Jake was standing there with his fists clenched.

"What are you doing here, Bonehead?" Jake yelled.

"Do you have a driver's license?" Nigel asked.

Jake seemed surprised by the question. "It's none of your business."

"It became my business the moment you hired me to level up your character." Nigel surprised even himself with his bold words. "Pull up that email from Pretzelverse."

As Jake whipped out his phone, Nigel went on to explain that a driver's license was proof that Jake owned the account and he needed to provide a copy to unlock his account.

"So, if I provide a copy of my license, I can get my knight back?" asked Jake.

"Yes," Nigel said excitedly. "Can I come inside?"

"No!" Jake snapped. "My mom is inside, and I'm not supposed to be playing games." As if on cue, Jake's mother appeared.

"Jacob," his mother said. Nigel recognized her as Martha, his mother's former co-worker. "I didn't realize you had company."

"He is not my friend," Jake said.

"Then who is he?" Martha demanded.

When Jake didn't immediately answer, Nigel said, "Tutor! I'm teaching Jake critical thinking skills."

Jake started, "Critical wh—?"

Nigel interrupted him. "Critical thinking skills are necessary for kids to learn subjects faster and with more depth. The ability for someone to think critically is important for today's job market."

"Oh, that sounds wonderful," Martha said. "Jacob, aren't you going to invite your guest in?"

"Uh...yeah, Ma."

"Great, I think we should work with your computer since there are a lot of great critical thinking sites I want to show you. Lead the way!" prompted Nigel.

Nigel followed Jake into his bedroom. As soon as the door was closed, Jake gave Nigel a big push.

"What was that for?"

"For making me look stupid in front of my ma," Jake said. "You basically said that I didn't know how to think."

"I had to say something to justify my presence since you blurted out that I wasn't your friend. And it worked. So now that we're here"—Nigel gestured toward the computer—"we should get that suspension removed. Shall we?"

Twenty minutes later, the task was done. Nigel helped Jake scan and upload his license. Jake received an email a minute or two later stating that Pretzelverse needed additional verification information, such as a utility bill, to help unlock his account. A driver's license was just one of the steps needed to complete the verification process.

The two stared at the email on Jake's monitor for what seemed like an eternity.

"Not a big deal. Can you get a copy of your electric bill, perhaps from your mother's desk?" Nigel asked.

"No! I'm not going through my ma's things for you. There has to be another way."

"I don't think there is."

Without warning, Jake started pounding on Nigel. Nigel yelled in pain as he took another blow to his chin. Nigel did his best to protect himself, but Jake was much stronger and just kept pounding.

After a minute—an eternity to Nigel—Jake threw him against the door and yelled, "Go! Get out of here. Don't let my mother see you!"

Nigel stumbled out of the house, holding his side. Nigel tried to ride home, but the pain was unbearable, so he resorted to walking his bike the rest of the six blocks home.

Shortly after Nigel arrived home, he discovered that Jake's account wasn't the only account that was locked. His account was also.

The Colossal Machine was rated Mature (M), for ages seventeen and up. The company had been making recent efforts to stop teenagers, including requiring additional account verification when an account looked suspicious and locking accounts. To get around the age problem, Nigel fashioned an online persona of a college student, age twenty-three, who attended a local university. Nigel needed to fabricate matching documents, find someone who could, or risk losing his account forever.

◻

Sitting in a small café, Len checked out the source code for the custom BOT program that he developed called Dark Glider. The purpose of Dark Glider was to help players with repetitive tasks within Pretzelverse's *The Colossal Machine*. Although *The Colossal Machine* was a giant sandbox where players from around the world could interact socially, there was a lot of structured content as well. For a player to explore the depths of a cavernous maze or navigate a jungle river, they needed to acquire skills, knowledge, and resources through prerequisite quests.

Len had spent many weeks perfecting the code that composed Dark Glider, and he had received a lot of praise in the beta testing stage. People were able to level characters and access adventure content in a fraction of the time. The café would be closing soon, so he needed to work quickly.

Len needed to launch the initial program before the expansion came out. According to his rough calculations, he figured he had at least a few weeks before that happened, perhaps longer. Normally, it would take one programmer more than a year to get a project of this size and scope off the ground. While Len was a good programmer, he had a day job, so he hired two additional programmers from an online working site called VDesk, one for the networking interface and another to hook into the game engine.

Word had already got out that he was creating an auto-leveling system for *The Colossal Machine*, so he knew he could sell thousands of dollars of product before Pretzelverse got around to changing things.

Len has been keeping his followers informed of the development of his mod on his blog called *Dark Happenings*. Although the official title of the add-on was CM Helper, the community dubbed it Dark Glider because he had often described it as a way to glide through the universe of *The Colossal Machine* as if on skates. Many followers wondered what the actual mechanisms of Dark Glider were, since much of the code was sent electronically to a private server on the Dark Web. However, most players of *The Colossal Machine* only cared that it would help them achieve their in-game goals quickly.

"There it is," Len said to no one in particular as he finished the last module for Dark Glider. After tonight's finishing touches, Dark Glider was ready for launch!

Len's heart was pounding as he clicked on the submit button that would send his changes back to the repository. There were a million other details to be done before he could launch Dark Glider. He hastily jotted down some notes.

- Send email to the marketing list
- Notify the community boards
- Web banner advertisements
- Final secure code review
- Tighten modules

As he left the café, Len pulled up his secure communications app on his smartphone and sent a message to his ghost coders: "Code complete when your mods are ready."

CHAPTER 4

JOHN APPLETON STARTED his day with a promising lead in the cybercriminal case he had been working on for several months. An encoded message addressed to one of the known associates that are connected to a cyber hacking group known as "The Collective" arrived in his office. The message originated in Minsk, which was not surprising since the group was active in Eastern Europe. He launched his secure email program, checked out the evidence, then ran the program to detect the decoding method. After eight seconds, the program listed the encoding type as "ROT-13." Luckily for John, this was one of the easiest algorithms to decode. It was time to deal with the big DD.

Marcus Sienna was the deputy director of the FBI's cyber command of the eastern United States. Janice, his secretary, was the gatekeeper for everything related to the deputy director. John was always polite and respectful of Janice's time. This kindness had gone a long way when John needed to see the deputy director on an emergency basis. Janice had been known to make agents wait a very long time before seeing the deputy director. She would prioritize the director's schedule, even if it was empty, to make an offending agent wait as long as possible.

"The deputy director will see you now, Agent Appleton," Janice said.

"Thank you, Janice."

"Have a seat," barked the deputy director. "What news do you have for us in Eastern Europe?"

The deputy director, also known as the DD, was often short-tempered with direct reports. He didn't have anything to report, so John felt a little better going into his office with some actionable news.

"I have a new lead on The Collective, Sir," John said.

"Go on."

"I was able to intercept an encoded message using one of the network taps that we have in place," John said. "We have them installed at several cybercafés in several suspected cities The Collective operates in. This one was in a coffee bar in Minsk."

"What was in the message?"

"I haven't had time to decode the message, Sir. I got the alert as I was commuting in. I was able to determine the encoding mechanism."

When the DD said nothing, John took that as a sign to continue. "The message tripped the alert because of metadata inside the message header. A person on a watchlist sent a message to known members of The Collective. We get these all the time, but usually the message is encrypted. This time, the message was encoded with the ROT-13 algorithm, which is significantly easier to crack than standard asynchronous encryption."

"English, please!" barked the DD.

"Think of it this way. Asynchronous encryption is similar

to a lockbox at a bus station. You put quarters in (your private key), then you take the key (public facing) out of the lockbox when you have enough quarters. When you have the key, you can unlock the locker to reveal the contents at any time."

"Can't you just pick the lock?"

"Yes, you can pick the lock, and you may get lucky and unlock it within the first few minutes. However, usually it takes a very long time to do this," John said. "Even with lockpicks. Or, you can break the lock with a hammer, but then you risk damaging what is protected, as well as drawing unwanted attention to yourself."

After several long moments, the deputy director motioned for John to continue.

"Encoding is better for us because the lock is not as strong. It's like a lock that protects a jewelry box. One strong tug and it's open," John said.

"This is all very interesting, Agent Appleton, but we need a solid lead. You shouldn't have wasted my time with this preliminary information," the DD scolded. "Is there anything else?"

"No, Sir."

"Then you better get back to it. The director has been on my ass, and we need a solid lead to move the investigation forward. Otherwise, we are going to shut you down."

"Give me a week, Sir. You will have your leads."

John left the office with an uneasy feeling in his stomach.

The popularity of Dark Glider took Len by surprise. He sold more than 2,200 copies during the first week. With each copy selling for $30, and after his fixed costs of $6,455 for programmers and advertising, he netted just over $60,000! Of course, there were other costs to consider, such as seller commissions for the services hired to handle his digital distribution and equipment costs. To add an extra layer of security, the seller offered payments be made with an untraceable cryptocurrency called Digibit. Len was skeptical at first since he thought it would hamper sales, but obviously this wasn't the case. If this kept up, Len might just be able to quit his day job.

Ellen was having a very difficult day. She had to hang up on two creeps and another customer who could only be described as belligerent. All she could think about was finishing her shift, grabbing some takeout, and heading home. She should be home in about an hour, but Chuck Stevens, her shift supervisor, almost always had some sort of surprise waiting for her toward the end of her work week.

Ellen looked up from her computer. Chuck was standing in her work area, and a little too close for Ellen's comfort.

"Ellie, do you have your weekly end-of-shift report for me?" Chuck asked.

She hated when he called her Ellie. Ellen suspected that Chuck was just toying with her. Ever since Ellen shunned his several requests for a date, he had been even more demanding and critical of her work.

"Reports are due at the end of your weekly shift," Chuck said.

"Well, technically they are due on Friday." Ellen usually finalized the report Friday morning, because she wanted as many extra calls as possible before her final shift ended. More calls meant bigger bonuses at the end of the month.

"That is only true if your shift is Monday through Friday," he said with a smug expression on his face. "You work Sunday through Thursday, so I want that report in my inbox by 6 p.m., or I will need to write you up!"

Ellen just sat there for a moment in stunned silence. This was the first time he asked for the report. Until now, he had always approved its submission on Friday. She would have to call Nigel and let him know that dinner was going to be late.

Nigel was in his junior year of high school, and though he went through the motions of getting essays written and sending them to colleges with acceptable video game development programs such as the University of Southern California (USC), or UC Berkeley, his primary focus was his video game side business. Ellen was constantly reminding Nigel that he had the responsibility of trying to get as many scholarships as he could so that Ellen wouldn't have to pay as much. At this rate, he may not need any tuition money at all. That thought scared Ellen more than any amount of extra night shifts.

At 5:59 p.m., Ellen got up from her desk and presented Chuck with a hard copy of her report for the week. He briefly glanced at it, then tossed it in his inbox dismissively.

"You can leave now," Chuck said.

The bastard didn't even look at the report, she thought incredulously. She immediately left without another word to Chuck. At least she wouldn't need to see him again until Monday. Gary would be in charge on Sunday. She liked Gary's management style much better than Chuck's, but he only worked weekends.

She called Nigel on the drive home from her Bluetooth-connected phone. Nigel didn't pick up. She called again about ten minutes later when she arrived at the supermarket and was sent to voicemail! She decided to just pick up a ready-made roast chicken for their dinner.

Every light in the house was turned off except for the one in Nigel's bedroom. Thursday was Ralphie's study group, so she didn't have to pick him up until after dinner. She dropped off the chicken, groceries, and her briefcase on the island in the kitchen, then walked upstairs, turning on lights as she went.

She knocked on Nigel's bedroom door.

"Honey, it's me!"

All she heard was a grunt. She tried a few minutes later after she popped the cooling chicken in the oven for a quick warm-up. Nigel did not respond, so she opened the door.

Nigel was sitting in the middle of the floor with his face in his hands.

"What's the matter, Sweetheart?" Ellen asked.

"Nothing!" cried Nigel.

"I think it is a bit more than nothing."

She pulled Nigel's hands away, and her heart sank as she noticed the bruises covering nearly half his face.

"What happened?"

"I got into a fight."

"With who?"

"With some kid." Nigel turned away.

They ate in silence. Nigel was clearly upset, so Ellen didn't press the issue. The moment he was feeling better, they were going to have a talk. She needed to set the record straight with her boy. After dinner, Nigel went to his room. Ellen didn't see him again for the rest of the evening.

CHAPTER 5

Nigel's heart pounded so hard at the mere thought of facing Jake again that his chest began to ache. A jumbled, unfiltered stream of data entered his mind: punches from Jake, Jet, his mother, the game—that cursed game! Nigel could barely swallow, and his thoughts were confused. *Am I having a panic attack?*

After several deep breaths, Nigel's head cleared, and he focused on finding solutions to unlocking both his and Jake's accounts. The Dark Web came to mind, but he had no idea how to gain access to the place where the shadows lurked. He couldn't think of any real solutions, so he did what anyone in trouble might do: call for help.

Jet was sitting at her computer (as usual), jacked into a remote section of *The Colossal Machine*, a premium section of the verse that hadn't been released yet. She was helping the game developers test for bugs and other problems in their new expansion.

Pretzelverse had sent her a large box full of goodies which contained a pair of bulky but functional virtual reality (VR) lenses. While the headset actually needed to be connected to her computer via wires, the immersive experience more than made up for it.

Through the eyes of the VR lenses, Jet noticed that she was on the top level of a tall silver tower. Her avatar had a long staff with a blue crystal at the end, and she could see it waving before her as if it were truly in her own hand. She activated her cloaking armor as she entered the metallic-lined corridor. To her immediate left, an oozing black sludge leaked out of several holes. She knew from experience that touching the sludge was an instant permanent death. She had many hours invested in her avatar and didn't want to lose her place in the queue by starting over. If any of the testers died in the game, they were immediately resurrected in a starting area with no equipment, and since it had taken her approximately forty hours to get this far, Jet didn't want to risk anything. She had limited time to play during school nights; her mother enforced a strict curfew on gaming. She had to be off The Machine at 9:45, and lights out was at 10 p.m., but it was only 7:30. Plenty of time to clear this level, gather her loot, and stash it in her hidden hovel.

She heard the chirping noise of her cell phone as she laid waste to dozens of minions the game was procedurally generating for her slaughtering pleasure. Since the game was online, she couldn't pause. She needed to reach the next checkpoint or a temporary safe camping area before she could even look at the text messages she was receiving. She couldn't think of anyone who might be contacting her at this hour. She didn't have many friends. She didn't date, either. She knew other like-minded classmates that might be testing, but most of them rarely used the phone; communication was usually handled by the in-game chat system. Her friends' accounts were "account-linked," which meant they didn't need to be online playing the same game to communicate. Pretzelverse had established its own communications platform that was truly impressive. The company could have sold subscriptions to the communications system to non-gaming customers. Jet didn't know why Pretzelverse hadn't done this already; it seemed like a good idea to her. She snatched a small peek at her phone as she entered into cloaking mode on her avatar's armor.

She picked up her phone. The message that caught her eye was from Nigel. It read, "Jet hlp 4 I T...STAT." Jet's heart skipped a beat when she read the next line: "I O U 4evr TIA." If a non-technical person received this text message, confusion might have ensued; however, Jet knew its meaning, a call for help. The first line translated to: "Jet HELP for I'm in trouble." The second line gave her hope, and the meaning was what motivated her to act: "I owe you forever and thanks in advance." Although this sounded innocent enough, when a fellow gamer sent the letters "I O U" together, it was a sacred message to the recipient. It meant that at any time the IOU could be called in for a favor of the person's choosing. Jet's palms started to sweat at the thought of Nigel owing her. She had sat next to him in class for a long time, and she was very fond of him. Jet quickly checked her inventory and found her recall scroll, which allowed her to instantly teleport to a previous location where she had been in the game. She cast the spell, then logged off in a safe place.

Jet replied, "Where do u want to meet?"

"Public Library at 8 p.m.?"

She lived about ten minutes from the library by bike and figured she better get going if she wanted to get there by eight. She replied, "Sure, 8 by the front."

"10-4. Bring your laptop."

The library was practically deserted. No one could be seen as she put her bicycle in the rack near the entrance.

Nigel appeared from the shadows. He was wearing a black

hoodie and blue jeans, and she could see his laptop in his hands.

"Hey," said Nigel.

"Hey, yourself." Jet didn't realize it, but she had a grin on her face.

Nigel smiled briefly but regained his composure. "Should we get started?" he asked.

Nigel led them to a table just outside the library and explained the Jake situation. Jet cringed when she heard Jake's name. Unfortunately, Jet knew Jake well. A couple of years ago, Jet's father got transferred to a military base just up the coast from Milford as a civilian contractor. During her first day at school, Jake made several unwanted advances toward Jet, which continued for more than a month. Jet liked to study outside the school gymnasium because it provided a semi-private, quiet area to study when it was too cold or rainy to practice. One day, Jake appeared out of nowhere and grabbed her by the arm.

"Get your hands off me, Creep!"

Jet shoved Jake back hard enough for him to lose his balance. As Jake stumbled, Jet spun around to flee, but another slightly shorter boy blocked her path. She attempted to run past when Jake grabbed her arm and started pulling her toward the gymnasium. She wriggled and almost broke free.

"Hold on to her, Donnie!" Jake yelled.

Before she knew it, she was in a darkened room. She had been so focused on Jake and his intent that she realized, too late, that the boys were carrying her to another area inside the gymnasium.

"Watch the door!" Jake said as he slammed it. Jake hurled her into an area that resembled a storage room. As she tried to get up, he pinned her down to the floor and immediately started kissing her.

Repulsed by his touch, she started screaming.

Jake backhanded her and quickly cupped his hands over her mouth. "If you do that again, I'm going to hurt you really bad, Bitch!"

He groped for the buttons on her blouse, but they wouldn't come free. Jet bit her lip and sobbed.

Is this really happening? Jet thought. At that instant, she heard voices.

"What are you doing here with the lights off, Young Man?" Mr. Robinson asked Donnie.

When Mr. Robinson got no response from Donnie, he pushed him aside and started flipping switches for the main gymnasium and adjacent hallways.

Startled by the change in ambient light, Jake stood up and attempted to flee toward the opposite end of the room where another door was barely visible.

Jet heard a loud crash. Jake was trying to move several tables that were placed in front of the door. Seconds later, the door of the storage room was flung open; it was Mr. Robinson.

Jet's vision blurred as the tears flowed.

"Jet, are you okay?" Nigel asked. He had a worried look on his face. She shook off the bad memory.

"Yes, I would love to help you with your Jake problem, Nigel," Jet said.

Nigel let out a small but meaningful smile.

"Since Jake doesn't want to give his information to Pretzelverse to help unlock his account, I'm thinking of finding an exploit of some kind to break into the account system. I read somewhere that there is malware, rootkits, or other software that can help me," Nigel said. "But I don't know where to look for them."

Jet didn't like hearing desperation in Nigel's voice. To her, Nigel had always appeared confident during their encounters at school.

"I think I have a solution that doesn't involve hacking and poses less of a risk than what you're proposing."

Nigel thought for a moment, then asked, "What do you have in mind?"

"A lot of people answering phones at companies give out information to people claiming to be someone else all the time," Jet explained. "After assembling a voice modulator circuit, you or I could sound like anyone."

Nigel was stunned. He never knew it was that easy to fool people.

"Have you done this before?" Nigel asked.

"Well, it's complicated!"

Nigel didn't want to press the subject.

"How do I get my hands on a modulator device?"

"I know someone who knows someone."

"Well then, let's get started," Nigel said with excitement in his voice.

Jet smiled in response. "It all starts with a pretext, a scenario that the person on the other end of the conversation must believe in order to obtain information or convince them to do something."

"A believable story," suggested Nigel.

"Exactly! You catch on quickly," Jet said. She winked at Nigel.

"Since we can't just make up a believable story on the fly, we need to set some goals. We need to ask ourselves some questions," Jet continued.

"What kind of questions?"

"We need to get Jake off your back. That is our main goal," Jet said. "Then we need to figure out the other details, such as the person we will be contacting and what information they will require. When you created Jake's avatar, what was his age?" Jet asked.

Nigel had painted a picture of a twenty-three-year-old college student attending nearby Milford State University. Unfortunately, that persona required some documentation they didn't have. Nigel would need to submit two forms of documentation, such as a driver's license, a utility bill, or a tuition bill. None of this was available, and forging one would take an enormous amount of effort.

"That is true for most people," Jet said as she smiled at Nigel. She didn't want Nigel catching on that she liked him, but she couldn't help it—they had chemistry. "We can find just about anything on the Dark Web servers. We just need to work out the details on price," said Jet.

"Should we go inside?" Jet asked. "There is little Wi-Fi signal here."

"I have an amplifier," Nigel said. "My friend, Milo, makes the best antennas."

"Cool."

"So you know how to access the Dark Web?"

"Sure," Jet answered.

"Really! Can you show me how?" Nigel asked.

Jet explained that a special piece of software called a Virtual Private Network (VPN) was necessary to maintain anonymity. A special web browser was also required. Once Jet tested the connection, she demonstrated the use of a browser called MORP. "The Multipoint Online Remote Privacy was developed by the U.S. military to protect covert communications," Jet explained. "The software is also used by criminals, freedom fighters, and privacy-concerned citizens."

"Okay. I need to either create fake documents to show to

Pretzelverse or hack into the electrical company for a recent bill," Nigel said.

"Both options are risky, but we should be able to create some convincing forgeries of an electrical bill," Jet said as she launched the MORP software. "There have been thousands of company breaches over the years, and Jake's mother's information is probably already on the Dark Web. Let's run a search."

Jet frowned. She only had three signal bars on her laptop. She needed at least four bars to create a secure, reliable, and untraceable connection.

"Is there a way you can boost the signal, Nigel?" Jet asked.

"Yeah, let me switch bands," Nigel said.

He adjusted the input gain on the radio in order to get more power to help boost his signal. He had to be careful because Milo said that the police often scan the area near public places for unusually strong signals. Nigel didn't think it was a problem tonight since it was a cold fall night, and he hadn't seen a soul on the street since he met Jet.

After some time, Jet handed the laptop to Nigel. He looked closer at the directory listing on the screen. The structure looked similar to that of a directory listing on a personal computer, with one exception. The file names seemed to be random strings of alphanumeric characters, all with the same extension: "un."

"What is this? It looks like random strings," Nigel said.

"The file names are purposely vague," Jet said. "Some of these files contain links to other sites; others contain information. It is hard to tell without opening the files."

"Is it safe to open?"

"It depends. These files can contain almost anything."

"Then how do we safely find the information without getting into trouble?"

"On the Dark Web, it's very easy to get your computer

infected if you click on any links or open the wrong file," Jet explained. "But there are methods to anonymously open these files, and to request information." Jet opened another window that contained a text document with several notes. "This is my cheat sheet. I had to write several algorithms to get it to work. I created a program that implemented each algorithm that scans and learns from each website. It's sort of like a search engine but on a smaller scale. I call it SpiderJet."

Jet chuckled as she said the name of her pet project aloud.

"SpiderJet is based on recursion theory, which is like peeling the layers of an onion. You see how each piece is put together as you unravel it," Jet said excitedly.

Jet searched her SpiderJet log for information about counterfeiters. She saw hundreds of hits in her saved index.

"Let's try one of these!" Jet said as she copied a cryptic link to her Scratchpad program, which allowed her to verify the link before going to it in the browser.

"I started using Scratchpad because I accidentally made a typo and got a very disgusting picture back once," Jet said.

Jet trembled slightly. It could have been the cooling weather, but Nigel didn't think so.

After verification, Jet was on the intended Dark Web site. It looked like the most basic web page ever. It contained only a few icons with some text below each one. The site's name caught Nigel's eye.

"Who names their website Ye Olde Info Shoppe?" Nigel asked.

"You see all sorts of site names here. Some have really rude names, so try not to get offended if you see any."

The first image displayed a picture of a driver's license with a caption which read, "Best Quality Licenses, any state for 0.516 DB." The second picture was a passport. What caught his eye was a picture of an envelope. The caption read, "Address Verification, any address in the US, 0.751DB."

"There." Nigel pointed to the envelope picture. Jet hovered over the picture with her cursor for a moment. A small window appeared with the word "safe." She clicked on the link, and a single page of links appeared. Nigel scanned the list for a moment before instructing her to click on a link that read, "Purchase Address Verification Service."

What appeared next was a generic-looking form that asked for several pieces of information, including a photo.

"Be careful here, Nigel," Jet cautioned. "You don't want to provide any personal information here, or anywhere else on the Dark Web, for that matter. You don't know who is requesting it, or if this site will provide you with what you want. We have to verify the merchant first."

"How do we do that?"

Jet pulled up another MORP browser window that looked like a discussion forum. "This site is called Dark Web Cred, and it allows users to post reviews on merchants and transactions."

After scanning these sites for the next twenty minutes or so, she finally came across some reviews for the site. Overall, the site had a score of 4.6. Not bad, but Jet had seen several other sites with higher ratings. She decided it was safe to use the site, but instead of using the form, she clicked on a nearly invisible link that read, "Contact site administrator." The link was pale yellow on the white background—very easy to miss!

Nigel was beginning to realize that attention to detail was vital when dealing with the Dark Web.

A new window appeared in the foreground with a textbox, reply address, and a send button. Jet typed, "Interested in product, need escrow service, provide escrow wallet address," and provided a return address of, "fountain_spade.leaf.un," then clicked send.

"It's done. When I get a reply back with a suitable DB wallet address, we can purchase the service," Jet said.

"What is DB?"

"Oh, I forgot to mention it. It stands for Digibit, a digital currency. Almost everything on the Dark Web accepts Digibit."

Jet glanced at her watch; it was nearly ten. "I've got to go, Nigel. Can we pick this up tomorrow?"

"Sure thing. Thanks again for all the help tonight." He smiled at her as she left, and his smile lasted for much longer than she was in his sight.

CHAPTER 6

EVERY MORNING, when Alexander Vandervoss drove into the parking structure of Prezelverse's northern Munich headquarters, he marveled at how much money it took to build. The main building was in the center of several other circular symmetrical buildings. The parking structures were located below each building so employees didn't need to brave the harsh winters. Like most technology companies, the buildings were not very tall, the largest being a mere six stories.

Underground paths connected each building so employees didn't need to go outside to get to the next building. Alexander grimaced as his cell phone rang. He hadn't even parked his car and the onslaught of calls had begun. He glanced at his watch; it was 7:23 a.m. Most employees showed up for work around eight. Alexander liked to get to the office early so he could get a coffee and check his email, calendar, and plan accordingly. He looked at the phone as he answered.

"Good morning, Brenna."

"Are you in your office yet?"

"No, but I'm nearly there."

"Please call me from your secure line once you are settled in the office. I have some news."

"Acknowledged," said Alexander as he terminated the connection.

Brenna was lead legal counsel for Pretzelverse Games, and she worked out of their Washington D.C. office. It must be urgent if she was calling in the middle of the night.

A few minutes later, Alexander pressed the button labeled *Brenna* on his desk phone. She answered on the second ring. Alexander looked at the LCD screen on the phone where the secure icon was displayed. Calls made from any executive line were always encrypted. As a result, certain audible artifacts could be heard; sometimes it sounded like modulation tones, or garbled gibberish.

"Hello, Brenna."

"I think we have a problem."

"What sort of problem?"

"An intellectual property breach as well as some trouble on the Hill."

"How bad is the breach? Did we get hacked?"

"Didn't get hacked, but Gregor noticed some anomalies on the code repository servers."

"'Anomalies on the code repository servers' sounds like a hack," Alexander said. "Assemble the team to meet at the cottage within forty-eight hours. Contact dispatch for help."

"Immediately—but we also have legal trouble with the U.S. Senate," Brenna said urgently. "A Senate committee has opened an investigation into the expansion. They are expected to vote on it next week."

"That was fast!"

"It usually takes months for a bill to get through the House and reach the Senate. For some reason, the U.S. Congress fast-tracked it, and voting was completed less than an hour ago," Brenna said with a very tired voice that Alexander hadn't noticed earlier.

"Deploy your team of lobbyists to Capitol Hill. I need you at the cottage in person," Alexander demanded, then immediately severed the connection.

Gregor's eyes were blurry as he pulled up to the cottage, south of Minsk on the edge of a forest. Usually the meeting was held just before the end of the quarter, but this one was held weeks early. Something must be going on.

The cottage had ten rooms and a downstairs basement area (complete with a World War II era escape tunnel). Alexander and Viktor occupied the downstairs basement section during emergency situations. The cottage was actually three houses interconnected by tunnels. Each home had several bedrooms and a basement.

Gregor practically sleepwalked into the cottage. He had driven nonstop from his flat in downtown Grozny. The drive would have taken a normal person well over twenty-nine hours; he did it in less than twenty-five.

Why didn't I fly? Gregor asked himself as he rubbed at his eyes. He estimated it had been more than thirty hours since he last slept.

He had to find Brenna. She was in charge of everything related to Pretzelverse official business. Gregor hoped the meetings would be brief; he wanted time to visit his girlfriend Dunya, a fledgling fashion model, in Kyiv.

Gregor was greeted in the cottage by Natasha, a principal member of The Collective. Natasha held positions on both the Pretzelverse and Collective boards—the difference was that Prezelverse was a legitimate business and The Collective wasn't. The Collective was in the business of fixing problems (not necessarily game-related) and had a stable flow of repeat business. Some of the more controversial clients of The Collective included politicians and business people with problems to bury.

"Hey there," Natasha said in Gregor's direction.

"Greetings, Comrade."

"You get me excited when you talk like that," Natasha said in a playful voice.

Gregor smiled in return. Gregor was a good-looking, tall man in his late twenties and was used to women being attracted to him. When it came to Natasha, however, Gregor always kept their relationship professional.

"Are the other members here?" Gregor asked.

"Da, everybody except you."

"Then let's not let them wait any longer!"

"Yeah, maybe we can have some fun later?"

Gregor just smiled as Natasha got up from her comfortable seating and opened the double doors.

"It was good of you to make it, Gregor," Alexander said with a hint of venom in his voice.

Alexander sounded really annoyed. *Or was it Alexei?* Gregor couldn't remember. He was so bad with names.

"My apologies, Comrades. Circumstances dictated that I drove for this meeting," Gregor said, taking a seat.

After a brief awkward silence, the meeting resumed.

"Brenna, what legal action can we take against the authors of this Glider tool?" Alexander asked.

"The authors of the tool appear to be unknown. Payment can only be made in Digibit through an anonymous store on the Dark Web," Brenna answered.

"Is there any way to dox the store owners or administrators?"

"I think that is a question for our late arrival," Brenna said as she smiled at Gregor.

"It is very difficult, but not impossible. I will see what I can do," Gregor said.

"Gregor, give us a status on the code repository situation."

Gregor explained that he noticed some unauthorized traffic egressing from one of Prezelverse's code repository servers. He traced the connection to a machine in California, near San Francisco, which was not surprising since Prezelverse did have a development office there. Although it was possible to access the server without a VPN, most developers didn't. However, the company did hire a number of outside contractors that didn't have access to a VPN. Gregor said he would file a report and have the IT manager fix the issues ASAP. The most troubling piece of news was from a connection in China; a large amount of data was transferred to that IP.

"The investigation results are still pending. I should have an update from my team by the end of today."

"You have until tomorrow morning to finish your investigation and provide a report. I'm surprised and disappointed that you haven't already," Alexander said.

Jet's house was a modest two-story. Its yellow and white paint was faded, but otherwise it looked in good shape. As Nigel stepped up on the porch, Jet opened the door.

"Right on time. Come inside," Jet said with a smile.

Nigel followed Jet to a back room filled with several games, a rather old dart board, and a pool table. Jet sat down at a card table in the back of the room where her brother, George, was already seated; Nigel gave him a nod as he took a seat.

"Good to see you again," George said. "Let's get started with this no-tech hacking lesson."

"I'm ready," Nigel said. "But before we get started, I need to know: How did you two learn these techniques?"

After a long moment, Jet answered Nigel's question.

"Our dad moves around a lot for work." Jet paused for a moment before continuing. "We would be placed in a new school every year or two. It would often take a long time before we got to know new kids. We would try and learn what we had in common with the kids we wanted to hang out with, build rapport."

"Did that work?" Nigel asked.

"To a point, but I felt that we were trying to get people to like us rather than making friends organically," Jet answered. "We did our homework on a target, a potential friend, found out as much as we could about that person, then struck up a conversation. Before we knew it, we had friends!"

"Well, we had people who liked us enough to do things for us," George said. "The key is to get your target to like you."

Nigel was listening with interest as George continued.

"This wasn't as hard as it sounds. If you like someone, they may like you in return. However, you can't fake it. If you don't truly like someone, it will be obvious to the other person."

Nigel had no idea that manipulating others in this fashion was even possible. He was thoroughly impressed with his friends' lessons. He planned to use these skills as soon as he could. The clock in the game room, which featured pool cues for arms and balls for numbers, read 3:35 p.m. He had been at Jet's house for nearly two hours and still needed to finish his pretext for unlocking his account. He thanked the siblings for their help and promised to relay his results.

Nigel checked his email: two more orders for high-level characters, and more for special items. He needed to get back into the game. Being the young entrepreneur that Nigel was, he decided to use another one of his backup accounts to continue his side business. He had to be careful since these backup accounts contained most of the rare and unique items that were sold separately. If something happened to this account, he would be finished.

As soon as he got the account back online, he received an in-game message from Jet. Nigel opened the message. It contained a scroll and a note explaining to use the scroll exactly at 6 p.m. She had some news to share. He put on his augmented reality glasses for access to the enhanced heads-up display the game offered. While it was not as immersive as the available virtual reality goggles, it did provide an acceptable enhanced hands-on experience. He could still move objects in a three-dimensional space, but he still needed his monitors to complete the illusion of immersion.

At 6 p.m., Nigel used the scroll to transport his in-game self to the location inscribed on the scroll. His field of view blurred for several seconds. When his vision cleared, he scanned the room for any signs of Jet. There was no sign of her, but he realized that he was in a sparsely furnished room that appeared metallic. At the opposite end of the room, two chairs and a small table were placed under a window. As Nigel took a seat, he caught a glimpse of the virtual horizon. In the distance, a mountain range with several waterfalls poured into a vast lake. At the nearside of the lake, a small sailboat was tied to an ancient-looking dock. Several animals which appeared to resemble unicorns were prancing in a nearby meadow.

"Hey, Nigel."

Nigel spun around. It was Jet, or at least the in-game representation of her, known as an avatar. Her in-game avatar appeared to be glowing. She wore a white robe and a jewel-encrusted staff. Her avatar put his lowly rouge to shame; he felt like a bum standing next to a queen.

"Let me guess, a mage?"

"Close, a Magi."

"Very nice! How did you pull that off?"

"By surviving the three trials and defeating the boss, of course."

Nigel haven't even seen any other Magi in the game. To become a Magi, the player had to possess the highest level of skill in the game. Nigel heard rumors of players taking months to obtain even the Pre-Magi status that is after reaching max level. He was in awe. There was more to Jet than he realized.

"Sorry I'm late. I had to deal with my father. He doesn't approve of the game."

"That's okay. I was admiring your microcosm." In the game, a microcosm was a private virtual space.

"Thanks. This isn't the only one I have."

"Really?" Nigel was impressed. Microcosms were not only expensive but rare because space was limited on the mega server.

"I brought you here because I wanted to discuss some potential changes that Prezelverse Games is planning."

"I know that an expansion is coming."

"As a beta tester, I have access to certain unreleased content. I've been authorized to share some of my experiences with a limited number of people. I think the changes will affect your side business."

"In what ways?"

"It hasn't been announced, and it may not happen immediately, but it will soon after. The bounty system is going into effect."

"Bounty?" Nigel looked worried.

"Bounties will be placed on anyone who uses unauthorized programs, or for anyone caught using any automation. That's not all—the dark denizens are being upgraded."

Nigel didn't like the sound of that. The use of even minor scrolls in the game had the potential of summoning a nearly unbeatable foe. "More powerful?"

"In a way, but they will be controlled by real players who can track the offending player. If that weren't bad enough, you can only access these dark denizens via a connection to the Dark Web."

"That is good. There will be less players," Nigel said.

"That is true, but anyone on the Dark Web is more advanced technically and will be almost impossible to beat alone."

"That is just great," Nigel said sarcastically. "Do you know when these changes will go into effect?"

"Not sure, but it could be any day. With the holidays fast approaching, it will probably be soon. Pretzelverse will want to maximize profits before year end."

"Thanks for letting me know."

"I would hate to have you waste your time leveling characters only to lose it all. The news was only part of why I invited you here. The final beta of the patch ends tonight, and each tester is allowed to bring in a guest. I chose you."

"I'm honored."

With a wave of her staff, she opened a portal. Jet urged Nigel through. Nigel stepped through the portal to find himself at the base of a silver spire. All of the pleasant scenery was gone; instead of prancing unicorns, there were flying gargoyles. One of the flying menaces took notice and started a downward descent. Nigel cloaked himself; one of the rogue's abilities was stealth. The creature kept coming. To Nigel's horror, he realized that the gargoyle could see through his stealth. Jet stepped through the portal, uttered some words that Nigel didn't recognize, and the gargoyle seemed to bounce off him. Nigel realized that she had cast a shield spell.

That spell is going to attract a dark denizen for sure, Nigel thought.

"I got you, Kid. Let's go," Jet said as she gave him a wink and a smile.

Jet led Nigel to the base of the spire. There was no visible door or entrance anywhere he looked. Jet uttered some sort of incantation which sounded like "Un-Por-Vet"—or something like that—and a narrow passage opened in the spire. Nigel followed Jet's lead. He could barely fit through. *More like a crack,* Nigel thought. Nigel followed Jet into a dark hallway. Judging from the mini-map on his heads-up display, Nigel suspected that they were on the ground level of the spire. Circular hallways led to unknown regions.

"Watch for sludgelings."

Nigel tried to say something, but it sounded like a grunt.

Nigel didn't know what a sludgeling was, but it sounded nasty. He followed Jet through the hallway leading upward. The walls shifted; it was disorienting to Nigel. He realized that it was a sludgeling because it stretched out and tried to attach itself to Nigel's armor. Jet cast another spell that lit up the room, which caused the sludgelings in the immediate area to flee. The effect only lasted a few seconds before they were back with greater numbers.

When they reached the top of the hallway, the sludgelings were covering every surface. Nigel checked his health meter for damage. He didn't take any. He realized they were floating. When they reached the end of the hall, the sludgelings vanished. A new threat presented itself. A large three-headed creature with fire emitting from the mouth and nostrils appeared. Jet shielded them but not before the fire from the monster touched Nigel; his armor had no protection. He realized that he had only one health unit left. He normally had a hundred units or more at any given time. Jet realized what was happening and cast a party recall spell.

Then there was darkness.

"You're safe now," Jet said.

"That was just a taste of the new content. Sorry, I didn't mean to take you that far. I got carried away. I patched you all up."

Nigel finally opened his eyes; they were back at Jet's microcosm.

"Was that the new content? I haven't seen anything that advanced in the game before."

"It is, but, unfortunately, most players won't get to experience it."

"Why is that?"

"It is some of the advanced Dark Web content I was talking about. You need special access to the Dark Web to even gain access to it."

"Can we go back?"

Jet smiled.

"I would like that very much, but I promised I would eat dinner with my parents tonight. My father is home for a change, and he wants to have a proper dinner, whatever that means."

Jet gave Nigel a scroll. "Have a look around before you go!"

After days of practice and coaching, Nigel was ready. He decided to start with his own account, in case there were unintended consequences. He spread out several notes he used when creating the narrative for the pretext. He worked out several responses and possible counters. He wanted to be ready for anything. Nigel worked on his pretext for an hour before he got the nerve to pick up the phone and dial the account resolution team at Prezelverse Games.

After waiting for about twenty minutes on hold, he heard a couple of audible clicks, and someone picked up.

"Player Support, Alex speaking," said the voice on the other end of Nigel's phone. For a second, Nigel said nothing.

"Is anyone there?" asked Alex.

Nigel cleared his throat. As he attempted to speak, he realized that he had forgotten to turn on his voice modulator circuit to mask his voice. He was reasonably sure that he didn't sound like a twenty-three-year-old college student. He quickly turned on the program.

"Sorry, I got something caught in my throat," Nigel said, regaining his composure. "I'm calling because my account got locked by mistake."

"Please provide me with your name and account information," Alex requested.

Nigel provided information on Alan Sommers, his twenty-three-year-old college student persona.

"I see that your account has been locked because two accounts were playing from the same source IP address at the same time," Alex said.

Nigel was ready to take a big risk. He chose his next words carefully.

"Was the other account Jake Hickham?" Nigel asked.

"I cannot reveal that information unless you answer a few questions. What is your address?"

"701 Front Street in Milford," Nigel said.

"What is the last four digits of the credit card on file?" Alex asked.

This was an easy one for Nigel since he created Jake's account and used an online prepaid credit card.

"5115," Nigel replied.

After a minute of silence, Alex explained that he would need to get approval to get the account unlocked.

"What is your relationship with Mr. Hickham?" Alex asked with a tone of suspicion in his voice.

"Ahh, he's my cousin," was the only thing that Nigel thought to say.

"Hold, please," Alex quickly said.

After a long pause, perhaps two to three minutes, the phone came back to life.

"Mr. Sommers?" said an unfamiliar voice.

"Yes?"

"This is Mr. Chambers, shift supervisor. As an extra measure of security, we require both you and Mr. Hickham to be present on the line before we can unlock either account."

"Oh," Nigel responded.

"I have his number on file. I can call him now, if you want?" Mr. Chambers said.

"No, that's okay. I think Jake is working tonight."

"All right. Please have Mr. Hickham on the line next time you call," Mr. Chambers said as he transferred the call to an automated survey.

Jake spent the better part of the morning doing research on Nigel Watson. He was able to find out that he had a kid brother Ralphie who attended Milford Elementary, just around the corner from Milford High School.

"Is there any other information you can find on the twerp, Donnie?"

"No, Boss. I asked several of my contacts at the elementary school, and that is all I have!"

"Fine. I need you to do something for me."

"A little fieldwork?" Donnie asked excitedly.

"Yeah, something like that," Jake said with delight.

At 2:45 p.m., the last bell for the Milford Elementary School rang. Ralphie was in the process of packing his backpack when a kid he didn't know bumped into him. The contents of his backpack spilled on the floor.

"Excuse me," the kid said.

"Ahh, look what you've done!" cried Ralphie.

The kid started helping him repack his backpack. Ralphie was distracted, putting papers back in his binder, so he didn't notice when the kid slipped a small circular disc into one of the outside pockets.

"Sorry, Man!" said the kid as he hurried away.

Several hours later, Donnie Davis met Jake at a local coffee shop a few blocks away from the school.

"Is it done?"

"It'll be days before he even notices it," Donnie said.

Jake pulled out his smartphone and launched the disc-tracking app paired to the smartphone. As Jake reviewed the logs, he noticed several gaps in Ralphie's activity.

"Donnie, I think the disc is broken. I see Ralphie at school, then he disappears until much later in the day."

"The disc is designed to be attached to a keychain or something else that is portable and will work with any cellular signal within thirty feet of the disc," Donnie said. "The gaps represent the lack of cell phone coverage."

"Oh, I see. Ralphie doesn't have a phone."

Donnie liked Jake, but he could be quite dense at times.

"Yeah. We will get better results if Ralphie gets a phone or is around someone that already has a phone," Donnie said.

"The twerp needs to hang around more people with phones. It's starting to get colder, which means he will get more rides from people with phones."

CHAPTER 7

To SUPPLEMENT HIS MEAGER INCOME, Nigel found some
helpful websites that acted as a work escrow service. Nigel
created a profile, passed several assessments, and wrote several
proposals. After monitoring the site for a few days, he lost
interest and resumed his unofficial character-leveling business,
but the money was starting to slow down now that players were
getting banned.

Nigel decided to find work in some low-tech areas. When
getting ready for school one morning, he noticed his mother's
copy of the *ThriftySaver* newspaper. It was folded in half, and
several advertisements were visible. He browsed the paper for
part-time jobs. Other than advertisements for mall Santas and
fast-food positions, he saw nothing he was remotely qualified
for. He flipped through a few more pages before an ad caught
his eye: "Hardware Hacking Challenge." Nigel didn't think he
possessed the skills for it, but he read on.

"Do you have a mind for figuring out the impossible? Do
you have the drive to figure stuff out on the fly? Can you think
outside the box? If so, then apply posthaste! Video interviews
will be conducted for the lucky few who can get through the
initial screening process. Pay is commensurate not only with

experience but the ability to solve the puzzles that I will set forth. The most successful candidates will have a mind for games, logic puzzles, and hacking (of course). One word of caution, my chums: If you don't apply yourself befitting to the level of effort that I deem worthy, then you shall be forever banned from my hacking-verse. Any accepted job that is not submitted within the agreed time will not be accepted, and the submitter will be banned from all future endeavors. A résumé, a written proposal, and a cover letter must be attached to each application. Any application submitted without these items will be destroyed.

"If you have the skill, drive, and desire, you shall be greatly rewarded. Bring a lackadaisical attitude or work ethic to the job and you shall reap what you sow."

The final section intrigued Nigel. He double-checked the age requirements—everyone over sixteen was welcome to apply, so long as they had a work permit if the applicant was under eighteen. The first requirement was easy since Nigel was almost seventeen. The work permit was a bit tricky since his mother would need to sign for it.

Since most of The Collective was offline for the evening and unlikely to return, Gregor decided to send a secure email to the principal members of The Collective.

Team,

I have confirmed that one or more Chinese IP addresses did have access and downloaded information from one of our development servers. However, it only contained development code which was not yet in production. What this means is that potential attackers did not access any working code or customer information. My team will continue to monitor the situation, and I will provide updates as I get them.

Gregor

Nigel started his day with the work permit weighing heavily on this mind. Fifth period was free for Nigel, so he decided to stop by the administrator's office to get more information on work permits.

As students began leaving fourth period, Jet tapped Nigel on the shoulder.

"How did the account unlock go?"

"Oh, the unlock is still in progress for my account. I think I messed up because a supervisor wants to talk to both of us at once now," Nigel answered.

"Let me talk to George and get back to you."

"I don't think I got to properly thank you for your help the other day, it meant a lot," Nigel said.

"Thank us after you get the accounts unlocked."

"Well, I've got to go. Let me know what George thinks," Nigel said as he walked out of the classroom.

As Nigel entered the admin building, he noticed Fred Rivera was manning the desk today.

"Hello, Mr. Rivera."

"Hey, Nigel, what brings you in to administration today?"

"I'm inquiring about a work permit."

"Okay, I can help you with that."

"Do I fill out an application or something?"

"The process involves one simple form and a grade check. As long as you have at least a B-average and a parent's signature, I can issue one," Fred said.

"How long does the process take?"

"Usually a few days. Remember, the employer cannot require you to work during school hours, and there is a twenty-three-hour limit each week," Fred said.

"Great! Thanks for your help."

Nigel stared at the login screen of the Collective Systems exam portal, apprehensive about taking the challenge. The test was designed to be taken only once. To prevent exam question leakage, each applicant was filmed during each exam. The test proctor was a live person that instructed the candidates on how to set up the room for the exam so no intellectual property could escape.

The proctors often asked candidates to move the camera around the room before the exam began. The proctors were given strict instructions. If the exam room preparation took longer than fifteen minutes, then the candidate was automatically disqualified.

As Nigel entered his username and password that was supplied by the corporation, the Collective Systems logo appeared on screen in a three-dimensional font. After a few seconds, the exam proctor appeared. *She is beautiful,* Nigel thought. She had blonde hair that was tied up so he could see her bare neck. For a brief moment, Nigel's thoughts started to wander. She was in her late twenties and had smooth skin and emerald eyes. *Is this part of the test?* Trying to forget about a beautiful woman was not easy for a sexually aware seventeen-year-old.

"I'm Natasha, your exam proctor for this session. Before we begin, I will record the standard legal requirement for this exam session. Are you ready?" Natasha asked.

"Yes!"

"Please read the text as you see it on the screen. I'm going to start recording, okay?" Natasha asked.

"Okay."

"Great! Now please give your legal statement. Read the text as you see it, no deviations."

Nigel took a small sip of water, then proceeded to read the text. Pretty standard legal stuff.

"Now position the enhancement camera we sent you in the line of sight of the camera on the computer."

Nigel fiddled with the camera until Natasha was satisfied with its positioning. He put sensors on his right hand and chest as instructed by Natasha. He was specifically told to place the sensors on his chest in such a way as to not reveal his bare skin. He could hear the shutter on the camera and additional motors while the exam proctor moved the camera around the room to find any blind spots.

"Stay still and look forward at the computer while I get a calibration."

Nigel felt a tingling sensation through the sensors which quickly changed into a slight burning sensation. Nigel immediately reached for the sensor on his left breast.

"Stop!" Natasha screamed into the microphone.

Nigel froze.

"Endure the minor discomfort," Natasha said.

Nigel's face contorted into a mask of pain; sweat began to pour into his eyes, blurring his vision. After what seemed like an eternity, all sensation ceased, and the monitors turned the darkest ebony. After a few moments, all screens came to life, and Nigel immediately saw a close-up of Natasha.

"Calibration complete. Are you ready to begin?" Natasha asked.

"Err, wait a moment," Nigel said as he put on his augmented reality glasses.

"Ready!"

Nigel felt his chest and groin areas tighten simultaneously. His head was spinning, giving him the strangest combination of feelings he had ever experienced.

As the sensation continued, he thought he was experiencing vertigo or having a panic attack. He lost track of this thought when his vision briefly blurred. The next thing he remembered was Natasha asking if he was ready. He answered, "Yes," but could not remember doing so; it was like watching a movie of someone else.

"Great! Let's proceed with the first challenge," Natasha said.

After a few minutes, Nigel began to feel like himself again.

"The first test is spatial integrity, which tests your ability to process three-dimensional shapes," Natasha said.

The screen briefly went blank, then a number of three-dimensional shapes appeared on the screen. Some of the shapes were standard geometrical shapes; others weren't.

"Now, reach out and attempt to interact with the shapes."

Nigel raised his right hand. Just as he did, he saw a hand appear on screen. He flexed his fingers and the three-dimensional hand on the screen followed. Nigel attempted to manipulate some of the shapes by trying to turn them left or right or flick them up and down. The exercise reminded him of one of the games he played as a kid. As each shape touched another, they appeared to stick. He tried to pull apart the shapes but couldn't. He realized that when the shapes finally touched, they would stick together like glue. He grabbed a couple of square blocks and banged them together; they repelled and started soaring fast through the air. When they touched other shapes, like triangles, they would slow; when the same types touched, they sped up. Nigel noticed a pattern. He tried to group the shapes so only the different shapes would be together. When he grouped some cylinders and circles together, an explosion happened and both shapes disappeared. He continued to group the shapes together until only a few shapes remained.

"Good job," Natasha said. "The next test will allow you to demonstrate your cognitive abilities. Test continues in thirty seconds."

Several shapes rapidly displayed, and Nigel was given a few seconds to match each pair. Other small tests measured numerical patterns, memory, and attention to detail.

"Excellent! You have done well on all of my tests so far," Natasha said. "The final test measures your ability to think critically."

"I'm ready to begin," Nigel said.

After another twenty seconds, all screens in front of Nigel went dark, then the next test screen appeared.

"Try to capture the largest numbers possible within the shape in the time provided. Test begins in ten seconds."

After the countdown, a group of numbers appeared in a nine-by-eight grid. Nigel did his best to capture as many large numbers in that grid within the given time limit. The frustrating experience lasted for several minutes.

"Final results will be available within a few days."

"How did I do?" Nigel asked.

"I can only say that preliminary results look promising. Thank you for your time."

Nigel awoke to the sound of his brother Ralphie playing a race car game. Although Nigel was six years older than Ralphie, they shared an oversized room the boys called the Loft. Ralphie thought the name sounded sophisticated and cool. Nigel could care less about the name—he thought of it as his sanctuary, since his mother rarely ventured into the room uninvited. Even with Nigel's eyes closed, he instantly knew the game that Ralphie was playing was *Kenny Kart*, a piece-of-garbage racing game with overemphasized character expressions accompanied by a meaningless cartoon soundtrack. Nigel preferred games with challenge, games that actually required a certain amount of skill to complete.

Nigel's mind wandered back to the rigorous series of tests that he was subjected to. The entire battery of tests lasted over four hours. Nigel was sweating all over after the exams were finished. The tests were nothing like anything he had experienced before. The woman with the blonde hair and piercing emerald eyes haunted him during his nap.

Nigel's line of thought was interrupted when Ralphie abruptly exclaimed, "Nige, you're up!"

Nigel ignored him and reached for his laptop. He must have been sleeping for more than three hours. He opened his email in anticipation. He had a nagging feeling that he didn't do so well. After waiting several agonizing seconds, he saw the message he was waiting for from Natasha at Collective Systems, Inc.

Nigel opened the message.

Greetings Nigel,

I hope this note finds you well.

You have been accepted for the Senior Student Researcher position. We feel that this position is best suited for your skills and abilities.

"I didn't apply for that position," Nigel said.

"What was that, Nige?" Ralphie asked.

"Nothing, Ralphie, just talking to myself," Nigel said.

You now have the option to assemble a team that will assist you in the day-to-day aspects of this position. You can recruit up to two additional people to help with these tasks. However, should you choose to enlist the help of others, they must be vetted and approved by Collective Systems, Inc. Since you are a student under the age of eighteen, we are required to obtain written permission from a parent or guardian. We also require a work permit to be issued by your school.

Nigel was particularly worried about this last part. He didn't think that his mother would be happy that he was applying for a job.

Attached is a formal offer and employment agreement. If the terms outlined in these documents are acceptable, please respond within 72 hours of receiving this email for further instructions. If you have any questions, do not hesitate to contact me directly.

Regards,

Natasha Solikov

Chief Recruitment Officer

Collective Systems, Inc.

After some thought and deliberation, Nigel decided to accept the offer. However, since he was underage, he had to produce a work permit. He decided to ask Natasha for guidance, but he didn't have her phone number. He could ring up Collective Systems in the morning but figured that an email would be best.

Dear Natasha,

Thank you so much for the offer letter. I'm interested in accepting; however, in the event that I cannot produce a work permit, is there any other position I can apply for? My school may take some time issuing the permit. How long do I have to produce that document?

Warmest Regards,
Nigel Watson

Nigel checked his email as soon as he got up the next morning. He received a reply from Natasha!

Nigel,

You have thirty days to produce the actual work permit. If you cannot obtain an approved work permit in this time, then you will be suspended from the position and will need to wait at least thirty-six months before reapplying to Collective Systems, Inc.

Regards,
Natasha Solikov

GREGOR BROUGHT up Pretzelverse's intrusion protection dashboard. The numbers seemed off, a larger than normal amount of inbound email was present, and there was an increase in outbound network packets.

"Damn! The stupid users are at it again," Gregor said.

From the patterns Gregor observed, it appeared an attack was imminent. Some stupid user probably clicked on a phishing link and got malware. Gregor sent a Cyber Advisory warning of the threat to IT and Network Operations. Better to let the grunts handle the details of chasing the malware. Gregor had more pressing issues, like collecting on a payday.

He retrieved a tablet from his backpack and looked at his own dashboard. His own phishing campaigns had been successful. Usually one user out of thousands clicked on any link. Last week, Gregor netted over one hundred out of ten thousand.

Gregor's red phone rang, his burner phone reserved for Collective business.

"Code word?"

"Sleeper."

"Connecting to Jaded Communicator," dispatch confirmed.

"We need to meet about our next move," Sasha said.

"Are you in Chechnya this week?"

"I'm at the cottage," Gregor said.

"Meet on level five in fifteen minutes."

Gregor was in the quiet study of the cottage. He approached the statue of Plato in the corner. He pulled the index finger on the left hand. The wall opened behind the statue. Gregor carefully stepped through the opening, which revealed a narrow passage.

Gregor pulled out a small flashlight to help navigate the small passageways located behind each room in the cottage. Gregor wasn't a very large man, so he could easily navigate the passage. He snickered at the thought of giant Viktor trying to navigate these tunnels. He would probably get stuck. About ten minutes later, he entered a large room on level five. Someone was waiting for him at the opposite end of the room.

"Sasha, that you?"

"Aye, come closer. It is difficult to see with just one lamp."

As Gregor came closer, Sasha appeared to have a large shadow behind him which reminded Gregor of a large, demon-like thing with talons.

"Have a seat. We need to talk about the vote," Sasha said.

"What about it?"

"I'm crafting a series of texts and will need your help with execution. I'm not a technical man, as you are. I've harvested a list of cell phone numbers that I got from your voter registration worm. It took some doing, but I finally got it to work. You need to provide better instructions," Sasha said.

"I will include a guide for dimwits next time. You have the numbers; what else do you need?"

"An automated way to send a message to all these numbers at the same time, and a way to not include a return number."

"Easy enough. What is your execution plan?"

"Send texts to young voters reminding them to use the eVote app during election day. Most young people in the United States don't want to be bothered with going down to vote, so I will leverage the eVote app. Users will download the app from the link that is sent from the text. They will see a voting form similar to the actual ballot in their state, but we will get so much more," Sasha explained. "The app contains the ability to track, record, and collect any information that we want. We can even limit the uploads for when Wi-Fi is active so their mobile data plans are not exceeded."

"That's brilliant!"

"I just need some help in execution. That's where you come in."

Ellen answered the next call that was in her queue. It was the last call before she could go to lunch. She was having a good morning so far and was two calls ahead of her daily quota.

"Telemarketers' Union, Ellen speaking. How may I assist you?" she answered in an upbeat tone.

"Hello, Honey," Rick said.

Ellen was speechless.

"What do you want?" Ellen asked. "How did you get past the screening process?"

Ellen felt her face turn hot; she felt flushed when she got angry. Rick had no right to invade her workplace!

"Calm down, Ellie."

Ellen needed to get Rick off the phone as soon as possible because her boss might be monitoring connections.

"Can I call you tonight?" Rick asked.

"No," Ellen said as she severed the connection.

Ellen looked at her small clock radio next to her computer monitor as she took her last call of the day. It was 4:40 p.m. The small display on her phone indicated that her average call time was ten minutes and fifty-two seconds. If this call fell into that range, she would get to leave early. She was five calls ahead of her usual average.

After her standard greeting, her caller identified himself as Chris and claimed to be from the IT department.

"Telemarketers' Union, Ellen speaking. How may I assist you?"

"Hello, Ellen. My name is Chris, and I'm from the home office."

"Oh, hi... How can I help you?" For some reason, Ellen immediately felt uneasy about this guy and couldn't put her finger on it.

"I cannot access the network in the Milford office, and I think I might have messed something up. I was wondering if you could help me test?"

"I'm not the help desk."

"Okay, but I cannot reach them and was wondering if you could help me out? It will only take a minute or two. I'm new here and have been out of work for a while, and it would really help me out if you could test something."

"What do you need?"

"Ellen, you are a lifesaver! Pull up a web browser. We have Internet Navigator here; do you have that?"

"We use a new browser called Corus. Are you familiar with that?"

"That's fine. Next, please go to CMHORG.org. It's a website for me to check on your connectivity."

"The site won't load."

"I see. Your antivirus may be interfering. Can you shut it off and try again?"

"We can lose our jobs for changing things on the computer," Ellen said. "And I cannot lose my job."

"I'm only suggesting that we pause it temporarily; it will reset back to normal at the end of the day when you turn off your system."

"Okay... How do I do it?"

"It's easy. Do you see a small yellow shield on the bottom right portion of your screen?"

"Yes."

"Right-click on that shield; you will see a small menu. Click on the pause option."

"Okay, that little shield turned red."

"That's normal. Could you please try to go to the website again?"

Ellen did. "The screen just turned red. That's it. I see no text or anything."

"Hmmm, that is puzzling. I think I might have really messed up your system now. Do you know the number of your local help desk?"

"Don't you have it?"

"The help desk in the home office is so swamped I cannot get in."

"Sure, it is 555-3487."

"Thanks, Ellen. I really appreciate the help."

Immediately after the call, she wrote down the conversation from memory; she was going to complain to Chuck about the lack of screening on these calls.

Ellen felt drained. Her head was pounding, and she felt like someone used it for drum practice. She locked her desk, quickly gathered her purse, and stopped by Chuck's office for a discussion about the mysterious caller. Unfortunately, Chuck had left for the day. It looked like his office had been unoccupied for quite some time. She remembered that Rick was supposed to call her this evening. She wanted to be prepared for that. She left the building around five. With any luck, she would be at home before six.

Rick called Ellen several times as she drove home. She didn't take a lot of calls from her car, so she never equipped her car with hands-free technology. The drive home seemed long and arduous for Ellen. She kept thinking about those damn calls! Ellen glanced at the microwave clock in her kitchen as she put her purse on the couch. It was 6:04 p.m. It had been twenty minutes since Rick's last call. She would not delay the inevitable any longer. She picked up the phone and dialed Rick.

Rick answered the phone on the first ring.

"It's about time you picked up your phone," Rick said.

"I don't have hands-free phone access in my car," Ellen said. "And I'm not engaging in unsafe practices for you."

No sooner were the words out of her mouth than Rick continued.

"I would like to pick up Ralphie this week instead of next because of a business travel conflict. I have a present for him."

"Ralphie's birthday isn't until next month."

"If we don't switch, I will miss it."

"Okay, we can switch weeks this one time, but don't make it a habit," Ellen said.

"Great! Thanks, Ellie," Rick said and hung up.

Ellen noticed a light in the next room. Nigel and Ralphie were probably looking for some dinner. She felt bad getting home late each night this week.

Nigel was making something in the kitchen, and Ralphie was setting the table! She couldn't remember when they last ate together as a family.

"Hey, Mom!" Ralphie said as he put down a stack of dishes.

"What's this?" Ellen asked.

"We're making dinner for you."

"You take such good care of us, we thought we would do the same for you," Nigel said.

Ellen stood in stunned silence.

"Have a seat, Mom." Ralphie urged her in the direction of the dinner table.

"Smells great! What's for dinner?" Ellen asked.

"Tuna Surprise," Nigel said cheerily.

About halfway through dinner, Ellen had to say what was on her mind.

"What's the special occasion?"

"Nothing special. We thought you could use a break, and with Ralphie going with Dad this weekend, we thought it would be cool if we had dinner as a family."

It sounded innocent enough, but Ellen knew her son better than that! She was sure he was up to something, but couldn't figure out what yet.

After dinner, they all watched some television. Ellen couldn't think of a better evening she had had in a long time.

Nigel was ready when Ellen called the boys down for breakfast. Nigel had the application for the work permit ready.

"Do you have to work late again tonight?" Nigel asked.

"Yes, Honey, I need to."

"I've decided to get a part-time job to help with things."

Ellen said nothing. She just stared at Nigel.

"It would be a help. I could buy stuff for Ralphie and me."

"Yeah!" Ralphie cheered.

"I don't think it's a good idea, Nige," Ellen said.

"Why not?"

"Because your grades are already suffering with all of the gaming, and I don't want to add to your *delinquency*."

"What if I promise to only game on weekends?" Nigel cringed as the words came out.

"That would certainly help your grades, but the answer is still no. I may reconsider if you bring those grades up."

Nigel looked down and said nothing for the rest of breakfast.

Nigel received an orientation email that provided very specific instructions on obtaining assignments. Although most assignments were given remotely, orientation for the position must be done in person. Each region hosted a quarterly orientation session. Natasha informed Nigel via text that the next scheduled session was this weekend.

"I don't have a work permit yet."

"Don't worry about the permit for now. You have thirty days to submit it," Natasha replied.

Rick pulled up at Ellen's house at 5 p.m. sharp. Ralphie jumped into the car. They waved as Rick pulled away.

"I have a surprise for you, Buddy," Rick said.

"Really? What is it?"

"I will give it to you this weekend."

When they got to Rick's apartment, Ralphie noticed several packed boxes around the house.

"Are you moving, Dad?"

"Yes, I'm moving away for a new job. Are you ready for your surprise?"

"Yes, yes, yes!"

"I know your birthday is next month, so I got you something that you could use now."

Ralphie frowned.

"I hope it's not socks."

"No, Buddy! Moms get those for birthdays. Dads get their boys cooler things."

Rick handed Ralphie a small rectangular box. Ralphie looked disappointed for a moment, and Rick thought it was Ralphie's disappointment of not seeing a game-sized box. But soon, that disappointment swelled into a smile.

"Cool! A phone!"

"A smartphone."

"Mom was going to get me one later."

Ralphie just looked at the box.

"What's the matter, Buddy?"

"It's opened. Did you get a used phone?"

"No, Buddy, I opened it so I could set it up for you. I added some games and some apps you need. The phone is not the latest model; you would need to be as rich as Eldon Tage to afford the latest in smartphones, anyway."

"Oh, okay."

Since Ralphie was the youngest, he often got Nigel's used things. Rick wanted to get him something new for a change! Ralphie immediately started playing with the device. Two contacts were listed, his mother's and father's, but Nigel's was missing.

"I didn't have Nigel's number; if you give it to me, I will add it to the phone."

Ralphie gave him the number without a second thought.

"Great," Rick said as he entered the number and handed the phone back to Ralphie.

Rick got out his phone and checked an app called Central Control Center, or CCC for short. He tapped the red dot labeled "Ralphie" and a menu appeared with several options. He tapped the record option.

Ralphie suddenly exclaimed, *"Kenny Cart* mobile!" and smiled at Rick.

Rick smiled uneasily back, waited a few seconds, then tapped stop. He immediately listened to the recording so Ralphie couldn't hear it. *"Kenny Cart* mobile!" said Ralphie's recorded voice in Rick's ear.

Nigel left early Saturday morning. His mother was off that day and liked to sleep in, so he left her a note.

Mom,

I'm going to be at a study group today. Please don't text, as we will need the day for intense study. Should be back before dinner.

Love,

Nigel

Nigel waited at a local coffee shop for the car that was to pick him up and take him to the orientation. Around 7:31 a.m., the car finally came. He had been waiting for over thirty minutes! The car was a black sedan with tinted windows. He could not see inside but had a feeling that he wasn't alone. The driver's side window opened revealing a rather burly-looking man in a black suit.

"Are you Nigel Watson?" the man asked.

"Yeah! What's your name?"

The man looked puzzled. "You can call me Rocky."

Rocky got out of the car and opened the back passenger door. Natasha was sitting in the back seat. Nigel stared for a long moment, until Natasha patted the seat with her hand.

"Have a seat, Nigel."

"I wasn't expecting you to pick me up," Nigel said.

"You've shown much potential. I wanted to make sure you had some time to ask any questions," Natasha said.

"Oh, that's cool," was the only thing that Nigel could think to say.

"You must have questions, Nigel," Natasha said as she rested her hand on Nigel's left knee. Nigel felt all the breath leave his lungs and pulled away reflexively.

"Sure, I have questions," Nigel finally said. "Why did you choose me? I mean, you must have had more qualified candidates."

"You did extremely well under pressure and scored in the 98th percentile of similar candidates. I wanted to tell you personally," Natasha said.

"Oh, that's nice!"

Nigel was disappointed by his lame answers, but his mind was working at half speed since she put her hand on his knee.

"You will have a chance to meet other student members as well as helpful staff that will help you with your new role. If you do well with your assignments, we may offer you a permanent position at Collective Systems. Consider this an internship."

"Can't wait!" Nigel said nervously.

A few minutes later, they pulled up to a very large estate. Nigel caught a glimpse of a stone sign which read "Tage Manor."

"Is this Eldon Tage's house?" Nigel asked.

"Yes, Mr. Tage is Collective Systems' largest shareholder. He likes to meet with all new recruits."

Nigel was treated to a spectacular view of the Tage Manor grounds as the sedan drove past the gate. Many kids approximately his age were getting out of various cars—none as nice as the sedan he was currently riding in. Instead of pulling behind the dozen or so cars that were unloading, the car veered to a side road.

"Mr. Tage is going to meet us at a private entrance," Natasha said.

Nigel was speechless. He was going to be meeting the richest and most influential person in the greater Milford area. Mr. Tage was a legend in Milford; he was descended from the original founders of the town. He was either a multimillionaire or billionaire, Nigel couldn't remember which.

The sedan stopped at a back entrance to the mansion, no less grandiose than the front.

Nigel stepped out of the sedan. Natasha was just behind him.

"This way," Natasha said as she led Nigel up the stairs.

At the top of the stairs, two men in butler uniforms opened two double doors in unison. Their timing was impeccable, as both doors were opened with mechanical precision. Nigel and Natasha entered a rather large room that appeared to be a study. Several heavily padded chairs and coffee tables were in the center of the room. Bookcases lined all other walls. Near the fireplace, two chairs were set at an angle so that people in either chair could see the fireplace and each other with little effort. An older man was sitting in a chair on the right side.

"He is waiting for you," Natasha said.

Before Nigel could say anything, Natasha was gone.

Nigel hesitantly walked up and stood directly in front of the man in the chair.

"Have a seat, Son. My name is Eldon Tage. Welcome to Tage Manor."

Mr. Tage pointed to the empty chair next to his.

"Can I get you a refreshment?"

"No, ahh...no thanks, Sir," Nigel said as he sat down.

"You are probably wondering why you are here and not with the others that arrived out front."

"Yes, Sir. I don't feel like I deserve such treatment," Nigel said with a nervous smile.

"Nonsense!" Mr. Tage said in a commanding voice.

Nigel immediately straightened in his seat, like he was being scolded.

"Listen here, young man, my time is important. If I called you to my private study, it was for a reason. You will do well to remember that."

Mr. Tage's friendly expression changed to something that frightened Nigel.

"You have scored higher than any candidate that I have seen in a very long time. You should know that I have personally met with only one other candidate with your potential. Your ability to reason and put together sequences of numbers is impressive. I'm looking forward to reviewing your work. If you are up to it, I would also like to set you to work on special projects for Collective Systems. You would be paid well."

"Of course, I'd love to!"

"Excellent. I look forward to our continued collaboration. You will report directly to Natasha. She is the only operative—I mean, employee—assigned to work with you."

"Thanks for your time, Sir."

"No, thank you, my boy!" Mr. Tage said as he stared at the flames.

Natasha next led Nigel into the Grand Ballroom, where twenty other students, age sixteen to twenty, were chatting, seated in chairs. Nigel scanned the room for an empty seat, but there were none left. Natasha took a seat near the front of the room facing the gathered students and waved him over. Nigel reluctantly took the seat next to hers.

"Shouldn't I be seated with the students?" Nigel whispered.

"No!" Natasha replied.

The room was silent for several moments. A six-foot-tall man entered the room dressed in a casual suit that looked quite expensive. The students immediately got up and applauded. Nigel started to stand, but Natasha made a motion to sit. The man in the suit addressed the crowd.

"Hello, my name is Alexei Breven. I'm the founder and CEO of Collective Systems."

The crowd cheered.

"Welcome to Orientation Weekend. You will spend two days of intense training on the processes and procedures of Collective Systems."

Nigel was alarmed. He left a note to his mother that he was attending a study group, not a weekend retreat.

"My mom thinks I'm gone for the day, not the weekend!" Nigel whispered.

"Calm down. It's taken care of," Natasha said.

Nigel didn't really hear what Alexei was saying and was totally unprepared for his next statement.

"Now, without further ado, let me introduce a young man

who has scored the highest on any Collective Systems exam. Please welcome Nigel Watson, our newest Senior Student Researcher at Collective Systems!"

The students applauded and cheered simultaneously. Nigel was incredulous. He stood and turned toward Alexei, who was waving him over to the podium. Nigel felt like he was walking through mud.

"Say a few words, Nigel," Alexei said.

"Hello."

"Tell us how you prepared for the exam?" Alexei asked, smiling at Nigel.

"I treated each module like a game and played until I finished the level."

"The exam is not a game!" Alexei said, giving Nigel a knowing look.

Nigel immediately felt uncomfortable; he took a deep breath before speaking again.

"I mean, I broke down each module and treated it like a puzzle as I solved it. I just visualized it as a game. I know it wasn't really," Nigel said.

The group of students seemed to hang on his every word. No one spoke for several seconds.

"Nigel used his skills as a problem-solver to guide him to the solution. Excellent work!" Alexei praised.

Nigel looked over at Natasha. She gestured for him to return to his seat. Nigel said nothing else as Alexei droned on. He knew he should be listening to perhaps gain a clue as to why he was up here in the first place, but he only heard the quickness of his own breath.

After the assembly, Natasha led Nigel to several other rooms within the manor. In one room, a group of students were working on machine-learning workflow on a whiteboard. Nigel was invited to try and solve their problem. The diagram listed several groups of information. One group was labeled "Filter"; another group of document-looking shapes was labeled "Classifier." Nigel asked if anyone in the group has considered a Naïve Bayes Classifier Algorithm.

"We have not," said one of the students. After a few minutes of intense discussion and computer searching, the group said that Nigel solved their problem. Natasha smiled as she led Nigel into another room and another. Each room had a similar group of students trying to solve a problem that Nigel had already solved in school.

"You are a genius," one student said to Nigel.

"Far from it."

The rest of the students laughed at his modest response.

At the end of the day, Nigel was led to his private quarters and given back his belongings. In all the commotion, he barely remembered handing them to Rocky. He checked his phone.

"Enjoy the weekend activities," and "I'm so proud of you," were the latest messages from his mother.

Nigel was clueless as to why, until he noticed a note left on the desk in his suite.

Greetings Mr. Watson,

I hope this note finds you well and in good health. Due to your recent outstanding scores in a test sponsored by Collective Systems, Inc., we have invited you to attend our annual retreat just outside of Milford as our honored guest. Your designated guide will be with you every step of the way throughout the weekend. Depending on your performance, several prizes will be awarded, including a full scholarship to the university of your choice. All students already have an internship at Collective Systems, where valuable work experience will be gained. We have taken care of all the arrangements for the weekend, including parent approval, so you can focus on your tasks.

We look forward to seeing you this weekend.

Regards,

Alexei Breven

CEO and Founder of Collective Systems, Inc.

Nigel awoke Sunday feeling a bit drained. The weekend took a lot out of him, and he still had several questions. The last day was riddled with more tests. More people that Nigel didn't know were present, and everyone kept asking him questions related to machine learning, many of which he didn't know the answers to. It was almost if they thought he invented it!

The weekend finally ended with a dinner. About halfway through, Natasha addressed the crowd of a dozen or so students.

"You may have noticed that there are fewer of you than when the weekend started," Natasha said. "This weekend was the final test. Those of you remaining have successfully passed and can consider yourselves full interns of Collective Systems."

Nigel felt both relieved and anxious about this development at the same time. He couldn't put his finger on it, but something was off. Something had been off this whole orientation.

"Different levels of internships have been assigned. Please open the envelope that is pasted below each chair."

Nigel felt for an envelope; there was nothing there. Every other student was opening envelopes but him.

"When I call your number, please line up," Natasha said.

Nigel looked around for numbers but couldn't find any. At

that moment, five people came into view, each with a giant number card.

Natasha called out numbers one through four. All other interns except Nigel were lined up.

"Each number represents a skill level. Your assignments will be based on these numbers until a new skill level is assigned."

Of the thirteen interns present, there were six Level Ones, four Level Twos, one Level Three, and one Level Four.

"Interns, please welcome our newest Level Five intern, Nigel Watson," Natasha said. She was looking directly at Nigel.

Nigel got up and stood next to Natasha. After the ceremony, each student was handed a packet and was instructed not to open the packet until they returned home. This was the last time that Nigel saw Natasha.

Nigel waited a very long time before Rocky came with the car. All other interns had already left with their respective rides. "Get in, Kid."

As Nigel got into the car, an overwhelming feeling of exhaustion came over him, and he fell into a comfortable sleep.

CHAPTER 9

AFTER A WEEK of planning in various internet cafés around Chechnya, Gregor finally decided on several small financial institutions. A large bank with millions of customers would draw unwanted attention, but smaller banks would not have the resources to track back as easily.

Gregor deposited the $7,002 worth of Digibit to cover the cost of the transaction. Seconds later, an encrypted file with digital goodies arrived. He knew that there would probably be some bad identity information in the file, but the seller had a great reputation in the online dark market community for having the best prices and merchandise. Gregor stood up and stretched. Time to get to work.

The room was getting darker. Gregor had to work quickly. The longer he sat on the identities, the more likely they would depreciate in value. He set his plan in motion. He wouldn't just assume the identities; he would own them. They would be owned.

"It's time to launch Operation Midnight," Gregor said to himself. He had a codename for each hacking adventure.

Several hours later, Gregor was able to liberate tens of thousands of dollars from accounts listed in the file. He opened lines of credit; it was too easy to buy stuff and have it shipped while "waiting" for the physical credit card to appear. His newly purchased items were on their way to several predetermined drop sites around the world. He crafted messages containing instructions for his network of mules responsible for picking up the items and delivering them to any number of Gregor's safe houses. The familiar glow of sunlight stretched across the horizon.

"It's time for Operation Midnight's cleanup phase," he said to the empty room.

He moved with the precision of a ninja, carefully closing all traces of his existence. The "cyber-warriors" on the other end had grown sophisticated over the years, but he still schooled them with the cat-and-mouse games he loved to play.

Gregor was living a double life, hacking at night and protecting his company's network by day. His head started to bob like a fishing lure, but he shook off the exhaustion as best he could. During these nighttime adventures, he would only get two or three hours of sleep if he was lucky, but for some reason, he seemed to do his best work when he was sleep-deprived.

At that moment, he couldn't remember the last time he slept. Had it been over forty-eight hours ago? He wasn't sure. Lately his employer, Pretzelverse Games, was under attack by all manner of threats. Most of the alerts were caused by gamers trying to break into the system using bot programs, and Gregor spent most of his time tracing down the Internet Protocol (IP) address of "script kiddies," called such because minimal skill is required to use their hacker kits.

One major difference between the script kiddies and a professional hacker was the point of entry and methods used. The script kiddies would start their attacks on the game servers directly. The professional hacker would always try to get in another way—through an open port on the email server, through a malformed script, via a phishing link, etc. The professional hacker was always looking for a payday, not access to the game servers to level up characters.

While there was some profit to be had selling fake or stolen game credentials, it was usually not profitable enough for the professionals—with one exception. If the professional hacker could get their hands on the key generator that produced the keys for access into these online worlds, then that was the biggest threat of all. This thought floated through Gregor's mind as he shut the lid of his laptop. He was starting to see double. He glanced at his watch. 5:32 a.m. He needed to rest before using the goldmine that he just acquired. *Only a few hours*, he told himself as he reclined in his chair.

"Bingo! There he is," Jake said.

"What are you talking about?" Donnie asked.

"The signal from the kid, Ralphie. He must have a phone. His blip has been constant since leaving school this afternoon."

"I believe this is the opportunity that we have been looking for," Donnie said. "Let's track him for another day or two to see where he is most vulnerable."

"Right. I want to teach the little twerp a lesson," Jake said.

Just after school, Ralphie retrieved his bike from the school lot. The chill in the air reminded Ralphie that there may only be a few more days of bike-worthy weather this year.

Just as Ralphie mounted his bike, a large hand grasped his shoulder tightly enough to hurt.

"Hello, Chum." Ralphie turned around and saw a large brooding man who looked more like an overgrown child.

"Who are you?" Ralphie's voice shook.

"I'm here to collect on your brother's debt."

"Who are you?" Ralphie cried again.

"I'm Jake, and I plan to take my $150 out of your hide, Little Man."

Before Ralphie could say anything else, he felt a punch in the small of his back. Ralphie noticed the kid who bumped into him last week during class. Jake pulled him off the bike and kicked it out of the way.

"Ahh! Stop!"

"Not until your brother coughs up a level-seventy character and my $150," Jake screamed. "Shut him up, Donnie!"

Donnie put his hand over Ralphie's mouth. Jake punched Ralphie in the stomach until he grew limp. Donnie's hand was wet with tears.

"Leave that boy alone!" called a man whose voice Jake recognized. It was Mr. Robinson.

"Time to go." Donnie and Jake ran until they were out of Mr. Robinson's reach.

"Emergency at the bike rack on the elementary side. Code red," is the last thing that Ralphie heard before passing out.

Ellen knew Martha Hickham well; they used to work together and were distant friends. Since Martha's son Jake seriously injured Ralphie, she felt she had to give her a call. Martha picked up on the second ring.

"Hi, Martha. Do you have time for a quick chat?"

"Ellen, it has been a while. Is everything okay?"

"I'm afraid it isn't. Ralphie has been attacked."

"Oh, my god, what happened?"

"This is going to sound awkward, but Ralphie said your son Jake bullied him."

"What!?! Jacob wouldn't..." Martha trailed off.

"Ralphie has no reason to lie. He said that my other son Nigel and Jake had some sort of disagreement. Do you know what that might have been?"

"Can I call you back, Ellen? I want to get to the bottom of this."

"Please."

Ellen's phone rang as she was making her grocery list.

"Did you confront Jake?"

"It took some doing, but Jacob finally admitted to harassing Ralphie."

"He did more than harass."

"I'm sorry, Ellen. I think we need to have Jacob and Nigel work their differences out."

"I agree. Ralphie is an innocent in all of this," Ellen said.

"I will talk with Jacob. I think you should talk to Nigel."

When Nigel noticed his mother's sedan was in the driveway after school, he instantly got a bad feeling. He heard sobs when he entered the house and froze in the living room when he saw his mother holding Ralphie in her arms.

"Now there, Mommy is here," Ellen said in a reassuring tone.

"What happened?" Nigel demanded.

"Ralphie was attacked today."

"What? Who?" Nigel felt the rush of blood flow through his face.

"Martha's son Jake. Ralphie was apparently attacked

because of something you did," Ellen said in an accusing tone. "I'm not a fool, Nigel. I know what you have been up to with your side business, and I'm putting an end to it."

Nigel's throat felt constricted.

"I also want you to refund Jake's money. Martha has assured Jake's cooperation."

Nigel said nothing. He only nodded in frustration and shame.

"Martha and I are expecting a resolution between you two by the end of the day," Ellen said cooly.

Nigel went to his room and immediately called Jake on his cell.

"Hey, Bonehead. How's Bonehead Junior doing?" Jake chuckled.

"Leave my brother out of this. If you have a problem, you come to me!"

"I tried, but you have been gone. I want what's owed to me."

"If I refund you, will you leave us alone?" Nigel asked.

"Give me $300 for my account and another $300 for Donnie's account by tomorrow and we will be square," Jake said.

"That's double the amount you originally gave me!"

"Then you can pick which one of you gets beaten until I get the full amount," Jake demanded. "Think of it as an interest payment."

"Okay, you win. But I need your word that you will leave us alone," Nigel said.

"Get me the money and unlock my account and you have my word."

Nigel could feel his smug smile through the phone. "I will need some time."

"A refund will buy you a week's worth of grace time, then the beatings will continue." Jake hung up.

Nigel took in a deep gasp of breath, then fell to the floor. His head began to spin. His vision blurred with tears.

After what felt like an eternity, Nigel got up and attempted to regain his composure. As he was wiping away tears, he noticed the large envelope that sat on his desk.

He pulled out a large folder that had his name on it. Under his name, the words "Senior Student Researcher: Level Five" were handwritten in elegant cursive.

The envelope contained an information packet detailing information about the internship, including procedures for rooting and sideloading applications on the student's smartphone and details on encrypted secure communications and how assignments were to be delivered via an app.

The last page of the packet contained scholarship information. To get the scholarship, students had to complete a minimum quota of assignments as determined by the level of the position. The higher the student's level, the more assignments were assigned. Nigel had a feeling the difficulty would also be higher. Nigel supposed he should have felt excitement, but all he felt was dread.

When Ellen went back to work, Chuck Stevens was in the front entrance of her office. He was chatting with the receptionist, a cute young woman in her late twenties. Ellen rolled her eyes. The receptionist was too young for him by at least twenty years.

"How's my favorite call girl?" Chuck said in a mocking tone.

Ellen felt the weight of his smile.

"I'm fine, Chuck. Thanks for the afternoon off."

"Is everything okay?" Chuck tried to feign concern.

"Everything is fine, Chuck. I need to get back to my desk."

"Don't let me stop you."

Ellen logged back in to the phone system but couldn't think straight. She should have taken the day off, and she would have if she didn't need the money.

Several hours later, she logged out of the phone system and made a list of items that was needed at the market. Ellen made a mental note to try to get more child support from Rick.

Ellen signed back in to her company computer and was shocked to see that she had a negative balance from overdraft charges.

A "bank transfer" of $999.99 got declined, but beneath it was another transfer of $899.99 that was approved! The next four lines of the statement were automatic debits and overdraft fees for a total negative balance of $36.86.

She couldn't believe it. She had no money! She felt stunned, confused, and angry. Someone had transferred money from her account! She would need to hurry if she wanted to get to the bottom of her banking problems; the bank was closing soon.

She arrived just in time. Only one other person was in line. She felt an urge to cut the line and demand to be seen, but she didn't think that was a good idea. The bankers were her neighbors and friends. Milford was a small town, and it didn't pay to be rude. A few minutes later, she arrived at the counter.

"Hello, Ellen," Joyce said.

"Oh, hi, Joyce. I have a problem," Ellen said. She felt disjointed, apprehensive, and angry at the same time.

"What sort of problem?"

Ellen's mouth was completely dry, and her thoughts were

difficult to express. "Someone made unauthorized transfers from my account."

"Let's look into your account." Joyce was silent as she typed. "It appears like you transferred $899.99 into your second checking account."

"I don't have another account!"

"According to the computer, you opened this other account online last Thursday," Joyce said. "We had a promotion; open an account with an amount over $800 and receive a $50 bank credit."

"But I didn't do that!"

"Your new account now has a zero balance. The entire amount of 899.99 was transferred to a Payfriend account," Joyce said, frowning. "The $50.00 credit shows as unavailable until tomorrow, since the credit promotion had a forty-eight-hour waiting period."

"How do I get my original account restored?"

"You need to transfer it back from your Payfriend account."

"I don't *have* a Payfriend account," Ellen shouted.

"Okay. I need to speak with my manager to do this. Unfortunately, Gordon, the branch manager, is out today."

"Is there someone else who can help me?"

"Not until tomorrow."

Ellen walked out of the bank in stunned silence. She checked her wallet. She had $13.48.

CHAPTER 10

NIGEL'S HEART sank when he saw his mother in tears. His mother was strong and rarely showed signs of weakness, so seeing her in a vulnerable state disturbed him.

"Mom? What's the matter? I took care of the Jake problem!" Nigel said. "Or, I'm *taking* care of it..."

Ellen composed herself. "Nothing's wrong, Sweetheart. I just received some bad news."

"Did someone die?" Nigel asked.

"No, Honey. I got hacked," Ellen said in a rather matter-of-fact tone of voice.

"Hacked? How? When?"

Nigel's mind was swimming. The Watson household was under attack, and Nigel was determined to find out who was behind it all.

"All I know is that my bank account was drained and someone may be using my identity. The bank has been useless," Ellen said, disgusted.

Did someone breach the defenses of our home network? Nigel left his mother and set out to find the culprit or culprits behind the hack.

⊡

Nigel pulled an all-nighter scanning his network for vulnerabilities. He did find an exploit on the router that his Internet Service Provider (ISP) managed. Nigel tried to patch it, but wasn't able to directly manage it.

"Hello, ISP Systems Technical Support. This is Marcy. How can I help?"

"Ah, hello. This is Nigel Watson calling."

"I see that you are an authorized caller, Mr. Watson. How can I help?"

"I found a major vulnerability related to your router and want to request a patch."

"Let me check." Marcy typed. "According to my records, your router's firmware is the most up-to-date version."

"No, it's not!" Nigel demanded. "The X11R has a major flaw that allows attackers to remotely control any system on the network. It was only discovered last week! Please check again."

"Our system is updated each Sunday. It's possible that I don't have the same information. I suggest that you call back on Monday," Marcy said.

"That is days from now. I need to protect my network," Nigel said.

Marcy didn't have anything helpful to say. Nigel slammed the phone shut in frustration. *How can a provider of internet service have such antiquated systems?*

Nigel woke up exhausted. As he walked downstairs looking for breakfast, he hoped his mother would be in a better mood.

His mother was crouched over the kitchen table, surrounded by jewelry, hands covering her face.

"Is there anything I can do to help?" Nigel asked.

"No, Nigel. It's my day off, and I need to visit the pawn shop."

"I will give you the money," Nigel insisted.

Ellen took Nigel's hand and wept.

"Thank you, Son."

Sally noticed that Ellen was not her usual positive, cheery self. Ellen's face had taken the form of a permanent scowl, unnatural on her pretty face.

"What is it, Ellen?"

Ellen just sat there and said nothing.

"What's wrong?"

"All my accounts are hacked, and the bank believes that my identity is stolen," Ellen said in one breath.

Sally hadn't a clue what to say next and was silent for a long moment.

Ellen's lips started quivering uncontrollably, and she started sobbing.

"There must be something that the bank can do," Sally said.

"Nothing. They can't do anything."

"I have an old friend who works at the FBI. Do you want me to contact him?" Sally asked.

"Really?"

"Let me put you in touch with him. His name is John."

"Thanks! You are a true friend," Ellen said.

"Don't mention it. That's what friends are for."

Ellen was able to get some food for the family thanks to Nigel's help. When she got home from work Sunday, she sighed as she looked at the clock. 7:03 p.m., long after Nigel and Ralphie's dinnertime. There was no sign of her boys, but she did find empty pizza boxes in the kitchen trash.

It's just as well, Ellen thought. Ellen was broke, even with Nigel's gift, but apparently Nigel had more saved so they could get some pizza. Perhaps she'd been too hard on Nigel for wanting to help with the finances.

She also needed to get in touch with her divorce attorney. Rick's last alimony payment was over a month late! At least he'd been keeping up with child support payments.

Her cell phone rang.

"Is this Ellen? This is Agent Appleton calling. Our mutual friend, Sally, gave me your information."

"Thanks for calling back."

"I need some more information from you. I have been tracking a similar case and want to make as many correlations as possible. Can I stop by?"

"Yes, please do. I'm at my wit's end here," Ellen said with genuine anguish in her voice.

"I will leave now. Give me thirty minutes."

Agent Appleton gathered information from Ellen's computer.

"So do you know how my computer got hacked?" Ellen asked.

Agent Appleton looked at her like she was a dullard; his gaze was intimidating to say the least.

"Not yet. I will need to give the information to our forensics guys. It may take a while," Agent Appleton said.

After the evidence was collected, Ellen showed him to the door, and he promised to be in touch. Ellen had an uneasy feeling about all of this.

Gregor sent an encrypted, high-priority communication to all members of The Collective. He found the true identity of one of the authors of Dark Glider, a frequent poster to many community forums that created cheats for *The Colossal Machine*.

"The real name of the poster who released the Dark Glider code is Len. He didn't have a last name, but I was able to obtain an address in Los Angeles, California."

Alexei immediately sent a response: "Please call me on my secure line ASAP."

When Gregor called Alexei, he sounded far away.

"How did you find the author of Dark Glider?" Alexei demanded.

"He got sloppy. His IP address was logged on one of the Dark Web servers. He must have forgotten to use his VPN, or the connection dropped. I have seen this before with people that think that the MORP browser will completely protect them," Gregor explained. "I was able to exploit the web server and download the entire connection log to find the IP. Getting the rest of the information was easy."

"Good work. I will get the team on this."

The Colossal Machine had been so popular that Pretzelverse Games had barely been able to keep up with maintenance, let alone create an expansion. However, Alexander Vandervoss insisted that one be developed. As a result, the main cadre of developers that led the original team were whisked away to a secret company retreat to develop an expansion for one of the most successful games of all time.

John Appleton read the latest subversive list briefings that were published surrounding any activity in Eastern Europe, where his main focus was Collective activity. A massive multi-player online game was hardly the focus of his day-to-day work, but he had a personal interest in games or programs that captured the imagination of the general public.

How could a company with a modest development staff release an expansion at this breakneck speed?

As far as John knew, the game had been out for a few months before the expansion was announced at the All Games conference in Southern California. One of the more disturbing aspects of *The Colossal Machine*'s expansion was integrating DNA samples into the game. One of the previous bulletins published about *The Colossal Machine* discussed the process in detail:

"Pretzelverse Games has introduced a new feature named P.E.T. 2.0, which stands for Personal Entity Tracker version 2. There is no official explanation of the acronym. Pretzelverse wants to convince pet owners to scan their pet's DNA into *The Colossal Machine*, to play with their pets in the virtual space. However, test players soon realized that they no longer owned the rights to their pets, their likeness, or even their names. They all became property of Pretzelverse Games."

The report continued with a highly technical explanation of the FBI's understanding of the process. John thought scanning and filing DNA was all pretty creepy.

During the beginning of their first break, Sally joined Ellen in the lounge.

"Did John reach out to you?"

"Yes, he came over last night. He said that forensic lab technicians will need to sift through the data on my computer before they can identify the hack."

"Oh. I don't know what was involved, but that seems a little extreme," Sally said. "I had another thought concerning your bank account."

"Oh?"

"I'm not sure what checking account you have, but the top tier account has certain protections against fraud. The bank calls it zero-liability protection, which means if your account gets hacked and it's not your fault, you *will* get your money back. It's worth looking into if you haven't already," Sally said.

"Thank you. That's good to know."

After her shift ended, Ellen stopped by the bank.

"I'm afraid that protection is not on your account," Joyce said.

"I have the Checking Premium account that the bank offers. It clearly states in the terms of service that I have this protection," Ellen said. She'd done her research.

"Let me check with the branch manager. One minute, please."

Ellen waited for the branch manager with a pang of concern. It was five minutes before closing. They better not even think about throwing her out.

After another ten minutes, Gordon, the branch manager, appeared. Ellen could see that he was scheming against her behind those round glasses.

"Good afternoon, Mrs. Watson," Gordon said. "I reviewed your account history, and you did indeed have the zero-liability protection when you opened the account. However, last spring we modified our portfolio and asked each account holder to affirm their coverages. I regret to inform you that since you failed to reaffirm your coverage, you no longer have this protection." Gordon gave her a sheepish grin.

"I never received any notice."

As soon as she uttered the words, she remembered some

flyers the bank had sent out. She had thought they were junk mail.

"I assure you that they were sent out. We gave you sixty days to respond. Since you failed in this capacity, we automatically unenrolled you," Gordon said in a monotonous drone.

Ellen took this as a personal attack.

"You people are incredible. You screw us in every which way with exorbitant fees, then when we need your help, you refuse! You people are *fucking incredible*," Ellen screamed.

Other customers were looking at her like she just escaped the nuthouse.

If Gordon was angry, he didn't show it.

"I'm truly sorry, Mrs. Watson. If you require a loan, I will personally authorize up to ten thousand dollars immediately."

Ellen began to calm down. She just wanted the nightmare to end.

"Thank you, Gordon, but I'll decline for now."

"If you change your mind, the offer stands."

Viktor enjoyed traveling to the west coast of the United States. He rarely got to see such nice and sunny weather. It took him over twenty hours to make the journey, but it was worth it to see the sun.

Len was at work when he received an alert that he had visitors. His security system was configured to track all movement around his home and alert him if someone lingered at the door or if a break-in occurred. Len looked at the security app on this phone, but saw no one. He tapped on the icons in the app to view recorded footage. He saw a man wearing a trenchcoat and a large-brimmed hat. It was a sunny but cool day in Los Angeles, and the person didn't stay long, so Len dismissed the threat.

Len always worked late into the evenings. He rarely took his work home, because if he did, he would risk the source code getting out. As soon as he finished, he headed home.

Len's front entrance was obscured by several plants and other vegetation. Remembering the alert, he felt a bit uneasy and briefly examined the app, which assured him that his home was safe. According to the app, all of the locks, doors, and windows were secure.

He entered his home and was relieved to find no one lurking in his living or family room. He turned the light on in the kitchen—and found a man sitting at the head of his dining table. He was tall and had a medium build but was not menacing. He was dressed exactly like the man in his security video.

"The boss wants to see you," Viktor said as he raised a pistol and shot Len in the neck with a dart. Seconds later, Len was out cold.

Viktor rummaged through Len's pockets, pulled out his wallet, and removed the driver's license which verified that his first name was Leonard, surname Stanovich. He removed his smartphone and launched the Collective Systems app. He positioned the driver's license next to Len's face so both were visible in one frame. Time to transport the luggage.

CHAPTER 11

ALEXANDER WALKED into the official research and development corridor of Pretzelverse Games for updates on the pet tracker project. He confronted the first person he saw.

"Hey, who's in charge here?"

"Who are you?" asked the technician.

"I'm Alexander Vandervoss, your boss!" Alexander snatched a glance of the name tag hanging from the technician's belt. "So, what do you say, Jackson?"

"Yes, please follow me, Sir!"

Alexander followed the technician down a series of hallways. Each major research area had thick glass walls that stretched from floor to ceiling in most areas. Most of the rooms contained technicians that were dressed in lab coats, and some had bio suits. Jackson abruptly stopped at a door marked, RESTRICTED—AUTHORIZED ACCESS ONLY, in large red letters.

"Try your badge, Sir."

Alexander waved his access card; the reader returned a loud audible beep and a red light flashed.

"Wait here, Sir."

"Why can't I go in?"

"It's your own rule, Sir, no tailgating."

Jackson used his badge to enter the restricted area and left Alexander to his thoughts. Alexander gained a little more respect for Jackson for challenging him to use his badge at the restricted lab. Alexander considered stepping up Security Awareness training.

A few minutes later, a rather tall man in a cowboy hat greeted Alexander in the hallway.

"Sorry to keep you waiting, Mr. Vandervoss. I'm Ron Allison, head of laboratory control."

The two men briefly shook hands. Ron motioned for Alexander to follow him.

"I think you might be more comfortable in my office," Ron said.

Alexander followed Ron down a few more hallways before Alexander entered a very sparse office. Except for several diplomas, Ron had no personal possessions in the office.

"That is quite the accent," Alexander said. "American south?"

"No, Sir. It is Texan."

Alexander examined the diplomas and noticed that Ron held a bachelor's degree in bioengineering from the University of Southern California and a master's in transgenics from the University of Texas.

"California for undergraduate and Texas for master's?"

"I've been interested in biology since my first frog dissection in junior high. I wanted the best education that I could afford," Ron said proudly. "I graduated *summa cum laude* from UCLA, and from there got the attention of other universities around the country. I chose the University of Texas at Austin to be closer to family. I'm originally from Abilene, but I figured Austin was in the same state at least."

"If that's the case, how did you make your way to us here in Munich?" Alexander asked.

"My son is stationed in Germany. He brought his family here, so if I want to see him more than once a year... Hey, you didn't come to have me yammer on about my education. How can I help you?" Ron asked.

Alexander was fascinated by Ron's background, as he knew few Americans with such dedication to their education, but he did have more important things to do.

"I came down to get a status on the pet tracker."

"When I saw that press release, I knew there would be trouble."

"Trouble? Please elaborate," Alexander said.

"I'm afraid we are still years off from execution of the pet restoration phase of the project. I mean, we have perfected the DNA acquisition process, but the restoration—or 'cloning' phase, as some would call it—needs a lot more work. I know the marketing department wants to capitalize on our work because I saw the preliminary marketing materials available on the Verse."

"Those are in development. You weren't supposed to see that yet!" Alexander said.

"Well, I think we have a permissions problem. If you don't want me in something, then I shouldn't have access to it," Ron said in a matter-of-fact voice. "I check the Verse daily for news about the company. I assumed that is why we have an intranet to begin with."

"You have a point, Ron, but rumor has it that you have successfully cloned at least one animal."

"At a great cost."

"How long did the animal last?"

"Only a few days. Even if we figure out a way to fully

restore the animal, the actual cost is prohibitive for the average person."

"How much?" Alexander demanded.

"Well over $50,000 per animal. It is much safer and more feasible to restore them in a virtual world. That was the original plan," Ron said. "Cloning in the real world is a more recent development. I had planned to include all of these details in my monthly report, but your personal visit preempted that."

"I need you to provide daily reports of your progress directly to me from now on!"

"What's the rush? We are moving as fast as we possibly can with my current staff and funding levels. We will get there in due time."

"Would it help if I could bring in another geneticist?"

"Yes, but certain tests just take time to complete. Our computers are simply not capable of running any faster."

"Let me worry about getting you faster equipment. You will have the geneticist by the end of the week," Alexander said. "Carry on. I will not take any more of your time," he finished as he left Ron's office in a hurry, leaving Ron to wonder how it was possible.

Alexei Breven sat in his subterranean office below the cottage. He pulled up The Collective's problem dashboard, which consisted of a listing of eliminations that were pending. Paid eliminations or threats to business operations had the highest priority. Alexei pressed the intercom button.

"Please send in Ioann."

A tall, physically-fit, middle-aged man appeared.

"Privyet, Alexei."

"How are you, my old friend?"

"I've been keeping occupied with some freelance work, which has been drying up in recent years. Not many have need for an old fixer like me."

"Well, I asked you here because I *do* have need of your services. There is something off about the organization," Alexei said. "I will pay double your normal rate. I need someone I can trust to take care of some wet work."

"I'm wrapping up a job now but can be available in a few days. Is that okay?"

"Yes, that should be fine." Alexei threw a rather large envelope in Ioann's direction. "This is a sign-on bonus. From now on, I'm your only client."

"Call in the interns," Alexei barked into the intercom.

Within minutes, Viktor received a call from dispatch.

"What is tollsgate?" the voice of the unknown dispatcher asked.

"It is a bridge," Viktor replied with the code word of the day.

The dispatcher confirmed that the code was correct, then demanded to know his present location.

"Just left American airspace, approximately 300 miles off the coast of Maine. Estimated arrival time in Minsk is ten hours with the Glider," Viktor said.

"Establish the Farstahl protocol."

Viktor had approximately forty-eight hours to initiate the Farstahl protocol before the boss came calling on him. Viktor put down the drink he was enjoying. Time to get to work.

Viktor headed toward the rear of the jumbo jet that was part of The Collective's private fleet. There were two compartments in the rear of the jet for storage and communications.

Viktor opened the storage compartment and saw Len, bound to a sleeping bed. Viktor could never sleep on planes; lying down on them always gave him nausea. He hoped Len was feeling nauseous.

"Enjoying your accommodations, Comrade?" Viktor said with a smile on his face.

"Who are you?" Len demanded.

"I'm the UPS driver, here to deliver a very important package to a very important customer. Now go back to sleep," Viktor said as he shot Len with another tranquilizer dart.

Viktor made sure that the package was secure, then shut and locked the compartment door. He entered the communications compartment. A barren desk and a seat attached to the floor were the only pieces of furniture. Viktor felt along the side of the desk and found the button that opened the compartment just in front of the desk. Viktor took the laptop out of the compartment, powered it on, and connected it to the nearest satellite. Viktor followed the instructions for the Farstahl protocol, then put the equipment away and returned to his drink.

Natasha located Bobby's Bar, a local haunt of Senator Wilson's. Natasha thought it was incredible how much cooperation a pretty woman got when she wore revealing clothing and tipped the bartender well.

After some discreet questioning, Natasha was able to determine that Senator Wilson was known to visit the bar on the second Tuesday of each month, which happened to correspond with Alice Wilson's monthly charity events.

Natasha observed the senator in action for about thirty minutes before she was approached.

"What is your name?"

"Gretchen," Natasha answered.

"What a lovely name!"

Natasha gave the senator an inviting smile.

"Scott is my name. I'm important in this town," Senator Wilson slurred.

During their conversation, Natasha palmed a small flask which contained a sweet-smelling perfume. Natasha was careful to dab a small amount of the perfume on her left index finger as the senator approached. As he turned his head, she put her left hand on Senator Wilson's face, then quickly grabbed his face with both hands and kissed him. For a brief moment, he looked dazed.

"Wow, that was great. What can I do for you?"

"Do you want to do something for me, Darling?" Natasha teased.

"Anything!" Wilson exclaimed.

"Give me your wallet!"

Senator Wilson reached for his wallet and handed it to her. Natasha briefly looked through the wallet and found some pictures of his wife.

"Who is this?"

"No one important. Do you want to get out of here?" Senator Wilson asked.

"Thought you would never ask," Natasha said in a playful tone.

The two of them left the bar and headed for Natasha's playhouse.

Nigel got the email early the next morning. The timestamp confirmed the message was sent before 3 a.m. It was from Collective Systems and was titled: A secure message awaits you. Nigel followed standard decryption practices. He needed to know the contents of the message before leaving for school. If it took too long, he figured he could skip a shower.

The message read:

Greetings Nigel,

I hope this note finds you well. As promised in your information package, your first assignment awaits. Reply with your acceptance if you wish to proceed with the assignment and details will be sent. You have the option to decline if the timing isn't convenient. You have twelve hours to respond.

Nigel didn't have to think long. He quickly typed, "I accept," then clicked the send button. It took several minutes, but he received a confirmation email instructing him to view the details on the Collective Systems app.

Crap, I forgot to install the app, Nigel thought. He didn't have time to install it now; it would have to wait until after school.

Ralphie was late for breakfast. He hadn't been his usual self since the incident with Jake. Ellen was worried about him. *At least Nigel was also more reliable!*

"How you doing, Honey?" Ellen asked.

"Fine. I didn't sleep well."

"Jake won't be bothering you again," Nigel said.

"Really?"

"Yeah, I talked with Jake. He promised to leave you alone."

Ralphie visibly perked up. "Oh, before I forget, I found this in my backpack."

Ralphie showed Nigel a small black disc. Nigel examined it closely. He remembered Milo talking about these once. *This is a tracking module,* Nigel thought.

"Do you know what it is?"

"I don't, but I know who does!"

"Milo?"

"Yeah, we are going to hang out after school. I will ask him about it then."

Alexei was awakened to an urgent call from Viktor.

"The package has been delivered. When do you want to receive it?"

"Immediately. I will leave now."

Alexei arrived at the containment area under the cottage where Collective detainees were kept. Upon opening the door, Alexei was hit with a rather unpleasant smell emanating from the package.

"Thank you for delivering the package, Viktor. Did you put the task into motion?"

"Yes, it is done. We received acceptance, and we are awaiting a response."

"Check for confirmation of delivery of assignment in another twelve hours to account for time-zone differences."

Viktor resumed his position at the door while Alexei got a closer look at the package. Len sat with swollen slits where his eyes were supposed to be, staring into the space in front of him. Alexei could hear short jagged breaths.

"What is the matter with him? Why are his eyes swollen shut?"

"Reaction from the tranquilizers. The doc administered medicine and said that he will be fine."

"You probably gave him too much. I need him alive and well," Alexei barked.

Alexei pulled a chair closer to Len; he wanted to savor the moment.

"Who are you people, and where am I?" Len asked in a weak voice.

"You are our guest," Alexei said. "I need for you to answer some questions. If I'm satisfied with the answers and you agree to our terms, then I will let you go. Is that acceptable?"

Len made a grunting sound, then nodded in agreement.

"Great! I'm looking forward to spending some quality time together." Alexei let out a chuckle.

Alexei walked across the room, found a very sharp knife, then cut Len's restraints. "No need for that! You are a guest in my cottage, and I want you to feel at home," Alexei said with a mocking tone. "Please give me your full name, email address, and home address."

Len choked when reciting his ZIP Code. "Water, please," he said in a soft voice.

"Oh! How rude a host I am. Viktor, fetch our guest a glass of water."

Alexei gave Len several minutes to recover before the questioning resumed. It took several hours, but Alexei was able to obtain all relevant details of the Dark Glider project.

"I believe you have given me all the information?" Alexei asked.

Len nodded in response.

"See to our guest's comfort. We will resume after the verification process is complete." Alexei headed for the door.

CHAPTER 12

SENATOR SCOTT WILSON was greeted by his assistant, Brenda, when he arrived at his office on Capitol Hill. "Brenna, the lobbyist from Pretzelverse Games, is here to see you."

"Send her away; tell her I'm in meetings all day."

"I would love to, but she is already in your office; she must have arrived when I was at break," Brenda said.

"Then I will throw her out myself."

When Senator Wilson opened his office door, a woman with average height greeted him with a warm smile and extended her hand. "Senator Wilson, thanks for seeing me today. We have much to discuss," Brenna said.

"I'm afraid that I'm double-booked today and running behind. Can we reschedule?"

"Sure. What days are you available?"

Senator Wilson opened the appointment book on his desk and flipped through the pages in his appointment book for almost a full minute. "I'm booked solid until January. Talk with Brenda about setting something up then."

"I'm afraid that will not do, Senator."

Before he could protest, she dropped an envelope on his desk.

"What's this?"

Brenna said nothing as he quickly scanned the photos which showed the senator fraternizing with a blonde woman at a bar. As Senator Wilson flipped through the photos, other more intimate photos of the couple presented themselves. In many photos, the senator was bound and gagged, with the blonde woman standing over him with a whip.

"Now do you want to send me away?" Brenna asked with a satisfied smile.

"This is an obvious forgery," Senator Wilson demanded.

"Feel free to have them authenticated by the local police, if you're certain that they won't circulate."

"You have ten minutes—but I need your word that these won't circulate, and all copies will be destroyed."

"Already done, as you hold the only copies."

Senator Wilson just scowled.

"I would like you to reconsider your position on the pet tracker bill. It has already passed the House. All we need now is Senate approval," Brenna said.

"The bill is immoral, indecent, and against everything I stand for."

"Ahh, I believe the bill is more decent than your positioning in these photos. I'm prepared to offer something in return, Senator."

"What can you possibly offer me?"

"For one thing, Pretzelverse intends to open a call center somewhere in the central United States. I believe it will create hundreds of jobs, something that your district is lacking. Also, your Senate seat is up for reelection. I'm sure you could use a generous donation to your campaign. Do we have a deal?" Brenna asked.

Senator Wilson said nothing for a very long time. "Yes, I will cast a yay vote when the bill comes to the floor."

"Thank you, Senator. Have a good day," Brenna said cheerily.

Sybold was a leading manufacturer of electronic voting machines and automated teller machines (ATMs). Independent security researchers had recently discovered vulnerabilities in both machines. Many banks that used the Sybold ATMs had made very public statements addressing how they patched the vulnerabilities; however, local and state governments had been slow to respond, if at all. Alexei's shadowy, off-the-books crew had purchased a number of older models of these machines in online auctions, gutted them, then sent the circuit boards to Gregor's lab at the cottage. Gregor intended to test these machines at various patch levels to see how vulnerable they actually were. There was embedded code somewhere on a chip, and Gregor intended to find it.

Viktor walked in, examining each piece of disassembled equipment with an air of authority. He looked like he was the one that designed it.

Damn it, he's here! Gregor thought. *Smug bastard.*

"Privyet, Gregor."

"How can I help you, Comrade?"

"I've come for a status report."

"My crew has mapped each circuit, and we are in the process of reversing the code."

"The boss is wondering why it is taking so long."

"Reverse engineering code takes time, especially when it's on read-only memory (ROM) chips. It would help if I had a schematic, but I've run into difficulty locating one for sale."

"We will obtain a schematic. You will have five days after that."

"By my count, we have twelve days until the vote, and I will need almost all of that time."

Viktor left the room.

Gregor could hear Viktor talking to someone in the next room.

Viktor came back and said in a matter-of-fact tone, "The boss has already dispatched Natasha to gather the schematic. She expects to have it by this time tomorrow."

"Great! I look forward to getting it," Gregor said, then added under his breath, "If Natasha was sent, apparently some persuasion was necessary."

Almost ready for execution, Sasha dialed Alexei to deliver the status of his plan.

"Hello, Sasha."

"It took some time, but I finally got the campaign back on track—no thanks to that lazy Gregor."

"I thought he came through for you?"

"Not quite. He got some of his crew to help, but they only came up with pieces of a vast puzzle. Viktor helped the most."

"Really? I didn't think he was that technical!"

"He isn't, but he is very methodical, which helped the process. Several calls to Gregor didn't hurt, but I could tell he didn't really want to help."

Sasha explained the campaign and execution to Alexei; he must have explained it dozens of times, but Alexei never seemed to get tired of it.

"Putting together a misinformation campaign is like creating a work of art. It takes time, patience, and love to ensure that it is well received," Sasha said.

"Indeed. You have my approval to proceed."

"Milo!" Nigel said as he waved him over.

Nigel was sitting with Jet at a back table of the lunchroom.

"Hey, Nige!" Milo said as he balanced his lunch.

"Need a hand?"

Nigel grabbed the backpack that was sliding down Milo's shoulder, making his lunch tray unstable. Milo quickly put his tray down, then took a seat next to Nigel.

"Why is your backpack so heavy?"

"Been working on a radio project." Milo opened his backpack and showed Nigel a large handheld scanning device. It appeared to be crudely constructed, and several wires were sticking out in various spots around the casing.

"What is that for?" Jet asked.

Milo looked at Jet suspiciously. Nigel caught the small but significant interaction between his friends.

"Milo, this is Jet. She is helping me with a school project."

Milo nodded.

"This is the antenna genius I told you about," Nigel told Milo.

"Pleased to make your acquaintance," Jet said as she held out a hand.

Milo smiled.

"Now I know why I haven't seen you much! Didn't know you had a girlfriend."

"Wha—no we are just friends," Nigel blurted.

Jet snickered and gave Milo a knowing look.

"I have something to ask you about," Nigel said, hoping to divert Milo's attention.

Nigel held out the disc he got from Ralphie.

"What's this?" Milo asked as he examined the disc.

Nigel watched Milo play with the disc. Milo turned on his

homemade radio-looking device and waved it around the disc.
A screeching noise emitted from the device.

"This appears to be a receiver of some kind. Where did you
get this?"

"Ralphie found it in his backpack. Is it a tracker?"

"Might be, but it responds to my signal tracker, so it is
based off of a radio frequency. I think it is an identification
tracker."

"Tracker?"

"Yeah. Its signal is strong when my signal tracker is close,
but when I move it away, the tones are faint, which means that
this requires a transmitter to be close by."

"Transmitter?" Jet asked.

"Yeah. It can be anything with a radio, even your cell
phone. Usually these work off of Bluetooth technology and
have a very limited range. I can examine it some more and let
you know."

"That would be awesome! Thanks, Milo."

It had been over six hours since Nigel received the message
from Collective Systems. The message would be expiring soon.

"Mom? Ralphie?" *Good, no one home. Need to sideload the
app on the phone, then confirm the assignment,* Nigel thought.

Nigel got to the bedroom he shared with his brother Ralphie
and emptied the bottom desk drawer to pull out the laptop
hidden there. He plugged his phone into the laptop, which
made it possible for him to install apps without the overwatch of
the app store. The process was quite arduous and required
specialized knowledge and software, but finally it worked.

"There, done," Nigel said.

"What's done?" Ralphie said.

Ralphie must have sneaked up on him during the side-loading process.

"Nothing, just updating my phone."

"Oh, I think my phone needs to be updated, too. I got all these texts asking me to vote."

"You got a phone? How?"

"Dad got it for me for my birthday."

"Let me see it."

Ralphie tossed his phone to Nigel. There were hundreds of text messages reminding Ralphie to vote. Each message was sent from a unique reply address, which made a mess of sifting through all the messages. However, the message that caught his eye referenced mobile voting.

"That's strange. You are way too young to vote."

"Tell me about it. The texts keep interrupting my game."

"Turn on your 'do not disturb' feature; it will stop the text notifications."

Nigel tossed the phone back to Ralphie as he continued to fiddle with his own phone project.

Cassidy's study session was interrupted by a series of texts which came in rapid succession. Cassidy opened the text from her brother, Milo, first.

"With Nige, be back before dinner."

Milo always does this, Cassidy thought. *He forgets about Husky, and I have to walk him.*

Cassidy closed her bedroom door and started looking for Husky's leash. Milo usually got home before Cassidy, and it was his responsibility to walk him. Alice, their mother, was very insistent about it, but Cassidy almost always covered for her little brother.

Husky was lying by the door, head drooping. The dog rarely messed in the house, but Cassidy didn't think it was fair that the dog wait longer than necessary. She hooked the leash on Husky's collar, put her headphones in, and left the house for an extended walk.

About twenty minutes into the walk, a series of beeps interrupted Cassidy's music on the phone.

"My stupid phone is exploding," Cassidy muttered.

Hundreds of texts were displayed on her phone: "Don't forget to Vote," or "Vote using mobile."

CHAPTER 13

ALEXANDER VANDERVOSS NEEDED to borrow some programming talent from his friend, Alexei Breven. *What Alexander wants Alexei provides*, Alexei chuckled as he pulled a red cell phone out of his desk drawer and dialed Viktor.

"Boss, how can I help you?"

"Pretzelverse needs additional programming talent. I need freelancers. I don't care about backgrounds or criminal pasts. I just need raw talent to help with a few projects."

"Consider it done. Please send the details the usual way."

"Thanks, Viktor."

Viktor orchestrated an operation known as Project Walled Garden. The project got its name because Viktor distributed the code via USB sticks within walls scattered around the globe.

Viktor picked up his red phone and dialed.

"Hello, Comrade," the voice on the other end greeted.

Viktor heard noises in the background. It sounded like a cocktail party.

"Gregor, are you sober?"

"Well, of course not. Why would I be?" Gregor laughed as he said this.

"Stupid drunk bastard! I will give you ten minutes to sober up and call me from a secure location."

Twenty minutes later, Viktor received a call from his red phone. No caller information was displayed, but he knew it was Gregor.

"Ready to work?" Viktor answered.

"Da."

Gregor sounded a lot better, and no distracting background noise could be heard.

"I have a crucial task for you. I will need you and your team."

"I see the details that you sent. It will be done, but I will need some time for execution."

"You have a week," Viktor replied.

After some considerable thought—a difficult task in Gregor's current state—he thought of how exchanges got done in the past.

Dead drops are popular with spies. Why not hackers? Gregor asked himself.

Ivan Kilosky tossed some chunky herbs into the mixture that he was brewing in a small cauldron. He hated using beakers and flasks when he could use an old-fashioned caldron instead! The caldron also held some sentimental value since his late uncle created it in Russia all those years ago.

He was working on a mixture of pheromone sprays that, in conjunction with Natasha's natural charms, gave her the edge that she needed. Just as Ivan was finishing this lovely thought, Natasha walked in.

"Natasha, my dear, please come in," Ivan said.

"Is it ready?"

"Not quite yet, but it's close."

"How long until it's ready? I need it, like, yesterday."

Ivan just smiled at his young associate. Her face had a cute wrinkle when she was angry. It was very subtle but visible. He thought she would need to work on that if she were to go up against an experienced agent.

"Come back in an hour," Ivan said.

Natasha stormed out of the room.

Ivan could have given her his excess supply of the pheromone potion, but he wanted to see her again. He finished pouring the remainder of the fluid into some vials, capped them, then picked up the phone and called her. He had her on speed dial.

"It's ready, my dear!"

Natasha hung up. Three minutes later, she entered the room with a cheerier appearance.

"Well, hello, Dear. It is so great to see you again," Ivan said.

"I'm in a hurry. I'm late for my flight," Natasha said.

Ivan frowned slightly. He knew her flight was at 3:58 p.m. It was just past twelve. It only took twenty minutes to get to Minsk airport from here.

"Before you leave, I need to explain the dosage," Ivan said.

He explained that the potion could be ingested with virtually any drink, but she had to watch the dosage with certain kinds of alcohol. Apparently there was an intense reaction when consumed with bourbon, vodka, or whisky.

"Jesus Christ, is there any drink that isn't affected by your potion?"

"No, just these drinks," Ivan said, ignoring the sting in her tone.

"Okay, thank you, Ivan. You are the best," Natasha said before she left the room.

Ivan was amazed that she could change her mood so

abruptly in such a short amount of time. *But that is the charm of Natasha,* he thought as he resumed his other experiments.

Alexei felt exhausted, like he was working two jobs. A phone call marked "Sasha" in red appeared on his phone display. Alexei tapped it.

"Alexei, Gregor's team really screwed us," Sasha said.

"What happened?"

"Many targeted text messages were sent to the wrong age groups. To add insult to injury, some phone numbers received hundreds of the same text messages."

"Was the source number shielded?"

"Da, all return numbers are randomized and will not accept return text messages."

"How many arrived at the appropriate age groups?"

"About 30 percent."

"Not good, but not totally bad either," Alexei said. "How many districts to go?"

"Half."

"Proceed. Time is not on our side."

"But what about Gregor? The quality of his work is slipping."

"I will deal with Gregor."

Sybold Systems' lobby was impressive for a company based in the middle of the United States. Natasha felt warm in the pantsuit. She preferred the silk dresses that she usually wore. She felt awkward and hot in this standard business attire.

"Can I help you?" the receptionist asked.

"Yes. I'm here to see Scott Davis, head of engineering."

After several minutes, a tall man with glasses appeared. *Disheveled appearance, wrinkled clothes, probably a bachelor,* Natasha thought as she sized him up.

"Mr. Davis?"

"Yes, and who are you?"

"Gretchen Roberts from Pretzelverse Games. We spoke on the phone," Natasha said as she extended her hand.

He shook her hand and went speechless for a moment as the tactile contact of the patch did its work.

"Excuse me, Ma'am," Scott said as he reached for his collar to loosen his tie.

"Are you okay?"

"Yes, fine. Come with me, please."

Scott led her to his private office and closed the door behind them.

"As you know, we are interested in potentially replacing our current hardware vendor."

Scott tried to pay attention to her voice, but he had a hard time concentrating. His vision blurred, and his eyes closed.

Natasha started her stopwatch app on her phone. She had maybe ten minutes before the initial sleep agent wore off. She hopped on Scott's computer.

Nine minutes later, Natasha was still attempting to locate the schematics when she saw a folder labeled "Proprietary Information." Scott started to stir from his brief slumber. She inserted the flash drive and copied the contents of the folder; she would need to examine it later. She composed herself and sat back down where she was.

"Are you okay?"

"What?" Scott slurred.

"You fell asleep."

"Really?" Scott sounded alarmed.

"Yeah, you must have had a long night partying?" Natasha said playfully.

"No parties... Can we reschedule?"

"Sure, Darling! I will show myself out."

Nigel opened the first message that appeared on the Collective Systems app:

Greetings Nigel,

I hope this finds you well.

Congratulations on receiving your first assignment from Collective Systems. The task below is tailored to your unique talents. To learn more and accept this assignment, click the "accept" button, otherwise click "decline." Remember, you only have a limited number of decline credits per month, and overuse of these credits may result in the dismissal of your internship.

Nigel quickly clicked the accept button. A few minutes later, details of his first assignment appeared in his inbox:

Debug the following code and send the corrected sample back via the secure app.

Nigel looked at the code. It looked simple enough, and the main module only had fifty-five lines of code. It appeared to be a module that was part of a communications system. There was code that referenced the Short Message Service that all cell phones understood.

Thirty minutes later, Nigel uploaded the corrected sample via the app. The annoying part of the app was that all code editing had to be performed within the app. There was no way to export the code to a computer, and no forwarding mechanism.

Several hours later, Nigel received a confirmation that his

solution was accepted and payment was sent to his Digibit wallet address.

"I want my account, now," Jake said as he grabbed Nigel by the shoulder.

Nigel wasn't prepared for Jake's bold actions in school.

"It's been more than a week, no account or refund! What gives?" Jake started to make a hand-pounding-his-fist gesture. Nigel flinched as he heard the smacking sound.

"Sorry, Jake. My mother was hacked, and I had to help her."

"I'm sick of your excuses."

Jake invaded Nigel's personal space and whispered, "I'm going to enjoy hurting you a second time. This is your last warning, Chum!"

"Do you have the Payfriend app?"

Jake pulled out his phone and checked. "Is this it?"

Nigel examined Jake's phone. The Payfriend app had a yellow exclamation point on it.

"You need to update the app."

"Done. Now pay me!"

Jake held the phone out to Nigel displaying a QR code which allowed him to receive funds from Nigel. After Nigel waved his phone in front of Jake's, the money was transferred.

"You still owe me an account," Jake said as he stormed off.

CHAPTER 14

NIGEL LAUNCHED the MORP program that Jet gave him so he could browse the internet anonymously. Nigel now felt relatively safe and secure; he could browse the Dark Web without anyone knowing about it. After about twenty minutes of browsing, Nigel found what he was looking for: the entrance to the dark compiler project called "Dark Glider." For a brief time, it was available for sale, but it was taken down before Nigel could obtain a copy of it.

He was about to give up when he spotted a forum post that gave additional clues. As he read through the posts, another black window with blue text appeared directly in the foreground. He attempted to click away from it, but it maintained its focus. Text appeared in the window.

"What are you looking for?"

"Information," Nigel typed.

"What information?"

Nigel didn't want to reveal too much information, but he needed Dark Glider.

"I seek the Glider," Nigel replied.

For a very long time nothing appeared on the screen. Nigel was about to give up and sever the connection, but he didn't want to leave his session in limbo. Finally, additional text appeared in the window.

"Are you worthy?"

"How do I prove my worth?"

Nigel didn't like where this was going. The person on the other end of the connection may be trying to dox him, a process of revealing someone's true identity on the Dark Web.

"Solve the challenge by playing."

"How do I play?"

"I will present you with a riddle. You must answer in the form of a question. Get it?"

"Yes, I'm ready to play."

"Excellent! I'm a function that is very aggressive; if I miss a prediction, my value increases exponentially. What am I?"

A timer appeared, counting down from sixty seconds in the top right of the screen in sixty-point font. The computer also started beeping distractingly after each second.

Nigel couldn't immediately think of the answer, but soon it occurred to him.

"What is exponential loss?" Nigel answered with just five seconds remaining on the timer.

"Clever, but you are not off the hook yet! What function is not continuous and impractical to optimize?"

Why are these questions all related to machine learning? Nigel wondered.

With only a few seconds left, Nigel typed in what he hoped was the answer.

"Zero-one loss."

He heard a loud horn sound, which startled him. No new text appeared on the screen for at least a minute. Nigel put his hands over his face. He was so tired of all this.

Almost on cue, he heard a typewriter sound emanating from this computer.

"You have skills and, therefore, are worthy."

A link appeared on the screen with a thirty-second timer.

Nigel clicked the link and stared in awe as the screen turned red with gold text.

Despite the hard-to-read colors, Nigel was able to download all three parts of the code—which was a puzzle in and of itself. The checksum sequence had to be downloaded in a specific order. The code also had to be assembled by the programmer who solved the puzzles. At the end of each puzzle (or test), a series of alphanumeric characters of varying lengths had to be written down or captured with a camera. Once all three sequences were gathered, the author required the programmer downloading the code to piece each part together into a single string, then run it through another algorithm to put together a hash. The programmer had to decipher the final pieces using an algorithm called ROT-13. Once each part was downloaded, the ROT-13 had to be entered to decompress the file structure.

A lot of thought and careful consideration had to be given to solve this puzzle. If the machine was cloned or virtualized, then Dark Glider would stop working. Even if the programmer was lucky and patient enough to solve all the puzzles, the decompiler had a limited life of sixty days. The programmer did not need to completely start over, however; a clue was given at some random interval between the original unlock and expiration. This clue was forfeit if reverse engineering (of any kind) was done to the program or source code.

"We have voting shills out there that are as American as anyone else at the polls," Alexander said.

"That is a lot of fake IDs and identities to maintain," Viktor interjected.

"If a voter's identity cannot be verified, then a provisional ballot is issued, which means we can control that vote," Brenna said. "These ballots are often reconciled after the election."

"Once we influence the outcome of the midterm elections, Pretzelverse's earning potential will increase tenfold," Alexander said.

"I've visited many managers at gaming retail stores who are planning launch events," said Sasha. "Many of the largest volume retailers have inquired about portable scanning units to be placed on site during these events."

"Great, but even if we don't have the capability of doing that, now we can keep up the hype by offering certificates or coupons," Alexander said. "I like it. Let's pursue this during the campaign."

Last night, Agent John Appleton had been examining traces of source code with little understanding of what he was looking at. John knew he could utilize code signature technology; he read an internal bulletin about it. Although he had no technical ability, he intended to seek out the agents that did. After spending the better part of an hour looking, exhaustion overcame him. He decided to take a break for the night.

The thought didn't come to mind until he was pouring his first cup of coffee the next morning. *I should start with the authors of the paper!* John felt stupid for not thinking of it last night. He hurried to his desk.

After a few keystrokes and mouse clicks, John was able to find the authors: Kyle Brennen and William Stohl. John started by calling Kyle. No response, and apparently he didn't have voicemail set up. He called William. No response, so he sent secure messages instead.

◻

The door to Len's cell opened, and the bright light irritated Len's eyes. He was squinting so much he could barely see who entered the room. It had been three days since he'd seen sunlight, or even another human being.

"Hello, Comrade," Viktor said cheerily.

"Did my information check out to your satisfaction?" Len asked. "Can I go now?"

"Yes, you are going somewhere, but it's not where you're expecting," Viktor said.

Len's eyes adjusted to the light. He saw Viktor standing over him with a wide grin on his face. The brief time he had known him, he had never seen him smile.

"Where are you taking me?"

"To meet your comrades, the ones who you created Dark Glider with," Viktor said.

"They're here?"

"Nyet. You're meeting them in spirit."

Someone from behind covered his face with a burlap sack. As it tightened, Len coughed as his lungs filled with dust.

Viktor chambered a bullet. Len heard the metal.

"I wasn't truthful before. There are others I worked with," Len said.

"I don't think so. The other two gave us all of the information we needed. They lasted a lot longer than you, I might add. Don't worry, I will make it quick."

Len gasped, a rather large oval formed in the burlap sack. Len began to shake all over. He crumpled to the floor. Viktor grabbed and pulled the burlap sack. He shoved the weapon into the widening gap that was Len's mouth and pulled the trigger. Viktor then pulled out his red phone and dialed.

"It's done. Dark Glider is no more!"

After a couple of sleepless nights, Sasha didn't have a resolution to his text message problem. He attempted to contact Gregor several times to no avail. He also contacted Alexei and Viktor, as well as anyone else who would listen.

Sasha's red phone began ringing.

"Yes?"

"Have you been able to locate the problem with your text messaging code?" Alexei asked.

"Nyet. Gregor has been no help, either."

"Well then, you are in luck!"

"What do you mean?"

"One of our interns fixed your code. I took the liberty of having it tested, and it works!"

Sasha was speechless. Gregor couldn't fix the problem but a kid could?

Agent Appleton was getting nowhere trying to reach either Brennen or Stohl. It was time to call in some favors.

"Deputy director's office," Janice answered.

"Hello, Janice."

"The deputy director is not in."

"I'm not calling for him."

"Calling in that favor?"

"Yes."

Janice sighed. She hated owing anyone for anything.

"What do you need?"

"I need information on two agents that are currently or were formally with the Bureau."

"Give me the information and I will get back to you."

After the successful completion of his first assignment, Nigel got multiple assignment opportunities every day. He was beginning to amass a small fortune in Digitbit, and he was also starting to become overwhelmed—not because the assignments were becoming more difficult, but because they were taking precious time away from helping his mother with her own hacking situation.

He told himself that he was helping by using the money generated from these ventures to put food on the table and gas in her tank, but the problem with working for Collective Systems was that he was paid in cryptocurrency, which was not easily convertible to cash. It was not like he could put in a Digibit ATM card and withdraw funds. The process he was using now took too long and required a lot of time.

Between working for Collective Systems, finding a way to automate his character-leveling process, and class projects, he was finding that there was little time to do much else. Nigel promised himself that he would analyze his mother's computer to find the hackers. The FBI supposedly examined her computer but had not been in touch since. The evidence was on the computer somewhere. He just needed to find it!

After a couple agonizing weeks, Ellen was starting to get her life back on track. She opened another bank account at the

Telemarketers Credit Union because she no longer trusted Milford Savings and Loan. The hack was over, but she felt uneasy about its lack of resolution. Agent Appleton was supposed to keep her updated, but every time she called he was in the field or otherwise unavailable. She had more faith in Nigel, who reassured her that he was doing everything possible to track the hack.

To prevent a recurrence, Nigel helped Ellen with new security measures. Ellen thought Nigel's security measures were a bit extreme, but she remembered what he said.

"Access to your bank account can be easy or secure but not both."

Nigel also noticed his mother's old computer sitting on the floor. His mother wanted to throw it away, but he advised her against it.

"I hate that computer," Ellen said.

Nigel knew that it wasn't the computer she hated but the situation that her vulnerable computer put them in.

"Well, we should wipe it properly, first," Nigel said. "Time to get the evidence."

Nigel carried his mother's tower up to his loft to start an imaging process that would not alter the original files on the hard drive. Nigel didn't have the necessary hardware to prevent writing files while imaging, but he did have access to a software version.

Thirty minutes later, he was performing a raw image of the original hard drive.

Securing a copy of the Dark Glider program was a big win for Nigel. Now he might have a chance of getting Jake off his back. Nigel's thoughts drifted back to the evidence on his mother's computer. He decided to multitask and set up Dark Glider to run while he was busy investigating the image.

Nigel inspected the contents of the imaged drive using open-source forensic software. Performing the inspection on the imaged copy of the drive reduced the risk of damaging the original contents.

Nigel ran a script that reconstructed all activity for a given time period on the machine. It was like running a time machine to go back and recover certain system activity, such as networks, internet browser histories, and what programs were being run. Nigel was hoping that he would be able to piece the clues together to at least construct a timeline of events.

Several hours later, Nigel found clear evidence of malicious activity on the computer. The hacker did a good job of cleaning up after harvesting his mother's information, but left one important breadcrumb for Nigel: an IP address to a MORP relay server.

Using an enhanced IP address tracker, Nigel was able to determine the attacker was operating out of Grozny, Chechnya —or at least the relay was—but he needed more information.

CHAPTER 15

NIGEL ASSEMBLED Dark Glider in the correct order determined by the ROT-13 clues that were given by the rouge site administrator. Nigel had no clue if these clues would work and install a dropper that would download malware, but he needed to act fast to level Jake's account. Nigel had to purchase a new game to proceed with the character leveling. The installation of Dark Glider required a node relay server to protect its anonymity. The easiest way to do that was to install the MORP node relay software. However, there were risks in doing that. There was a slight possibility that it could be traced back to Nigel. *What if I set Jake up with this capability?*

If Nigel were able to set up Jake with a way to level his character himself, he would be off the hook and wouldn't need to take any more risks with Jake. All it took was a little hardware, which he had, and some time. Nigel picked up his phone and dialed.

"Hey, I didn't expect to hear from you so soon. You have my level seventy?" Jake asked.

"I do, in a manner of speaking."

"What?"

"We need to set up something at your place for it to work,

not only will you have a level-seventy character, you will have the ability to create your own items and hunt other players. Jake, you there?"

"Yeah. What's the catch?"

"No catch. You need to promise not to ever contact me or my family again. Deal?"

"Yeah, come over."

Nigel grabbed a few miscellaneous items to make Dark Glider work with the relay server. He had a small project board kit he had assembled last summer. It wasn't powerful enough to play games, but would serve nicely as a MORP node relay.

About an hour later, Nigel showed up at Jake's house with his gear. It took some downloading, installing, and some configuration, but his new MORP dark node relay was ready.

"Is my leveling box ready?"

"Almost, still have to do some finishing touches. Do you know how to access your router's configuration?"

Based on the blank expression that Jake emanated, Nigel decided that he had no clue what Nigel was saying.

"Never mind. I need to get on your computer to finish."

Jake pointed at the computer.

Nigel visited a website to get detailed information from Jake's internet provider. *He uses the same provider as me. Perfect.* From experience, Nigel knew the default authentication credentials for Jake's router. He was in.

Jake really needs to change from the default credentials.

A few minutes later, Nigel obtained Jake's IP address that was reserved for Jake's house and added it to the MORP relay server configuration. Nigel also placed Dark Glider in the "Colossal Machine Mods" folder.

"Done!" Nigel said.

"Can I level my character now?"

"Let's try."

Nigel loaded *The Colossal Machine* game, entered the username and password he created for Jake, and Jake's level-five avatar appeared.

"Notice that you are level five still? This is going to change."

"Hell ya."

Nigel used a keyboard shortcut command to bring up a text-based menu with information such as location, coordinates, modifications, and other metadata. Nigel typed in the following to activate Dark Glider:

"Load Dark_Glider wit full fury 10.10.1.1 admin changeme."

This command specified to *The Colossal Machine* that the Dark Glider was loading with his IP and credentials to the MORP relay server. *The Colossal Machine* wasn't supposed to work with code from another machine, but Dark Glider took advantage of an unpatched vulnerability in *The Colossal Machine* to connect to the MORP relay to hide Jake's unauthorized use of Dark Glider.

The add-on appeared to be working because he noticed the menu bar where text commands were entered was different. "<I shall serve my lord:>" was displayed.

Nigel typed, "Initiate accelerate mode level five."

"Now play your avatar, Jake," Nigel said.

Jake started playing the character. He immediately started killing things like boars, dogs, cats, and anything that he could use his virtual sword to whack.

"I kill so easily now," Jake said.

"Yeah, and that's not all."

Jake's sword broke as he was indiscriminately killing everything.

"No worries. Allow me."

Nigel reached over Jake's shoulder and tapped in some

commands. Jake's sword was instantly fixed.

Jake just stared, dumbfounded.

"This is awesome!" Jake yelled.

"With the power of the server box, I installed your powers off the add-on. You will reign supreme, but there is one glitch."

"What's that?"

"You need to limit yourself to ten levels per day. You also need to move around in the game world, a lot. This is to protect yourself against being found out by the game monitors."

"Got it."

Nigel didn't make a move to leave.

"We are finished. I will leave you and your brother alone. Now beat it, Bonehead."

Nigel turned to leave, then stopped short of the door.

"One other thing. This is important."

"What is it?" Jake said as he was killing things.

"You need to keep your MORP software patched."

"Oh, sure."

Jake waved a hand toward the door.

"What am I missing?" Alexei asked.

"What do you mean?" Gregor countered.

"I thought you were the best! I guess I was wrong because one of our interns solved something that you couldn't."

"What are you talking about?"

"Sasha's communication program—developed by *you*—had several bugs that almost compromised the operation, and apparently you wouldn't or couldn't help him!"

"I was very busy and—"

"That doesn't cut it," Alexei cut Gregor off, looking at him in disgust. "I'm putting you on probation. Perhaps I will replace you with the kid. Now get out of my sight."

Agent Appleton's phone rang.

"I found the locations of the agents," Janice said. "Kyle Brennen is retired."

"Can I get his contact information? I need to speak with him."

"You don't understand—by retired, I mean deceased," Janice admitted.

"What about Stohl?"

"Relocated and reallocated."

"What does *that* mean?"

"Didn't anyone at the Bureau teach you anything? Stohl got reassigned to another agency. His name was changed, and he moved to protect his identity," Janice explained, as if to a child.

"Can you at least provide me with the new name and location?"

After a long silence, Janice spoke again. "I can lose my job for this! But I owe you a debt that is difficult to repay. Henry is the only name I could find."

Agent Appleton thanked Janice for her help. Time to pay Milford another visit.

It was irrational, but Gregor was beginning to feel threatened by Nigel. In truth, Nigel reminded Gregor of himself ten years prior. Alexei had hand-picked Gregor from a recruiting event in Eastern Europe.

After some preliminary research and database manipulation, Gregor was able to locate the HR database that contained basic employee information. From there, he loaded his exploit program called Datasploit and looked for the exploit module needed to successfully access the database.

Five minutes later, Gregor was able to gain access to Nigel's file. After a preliminary scan, he noticed Nigel was interestingly from the same American town that contained the bank he recently hacked.

Gregor clicked on the "Metadata" tab. After a few seconds, several groups of text blocks were visible on the screen. One heading read "VPN," another "HomeNet." Other blocks were labeled "CoffeeNet," "AirNet," and "GameNet." Gregor clicked on the HomeNet grouping, and each of the blocks expanded into an interconnected network. Each block was connected by keywords in a block called a primary key.

Several pieces of information appeared once Gregor clicked on the HomeNet image. One block was labeled "pictures," another called "code"; however, one block that particularly caught his eye was labeled "known associates." Immediately, four other blocks appeared, each with a name. Each of the names had one or more other blocks, depending on the level of interaction. He noticed blocks labeled "Jet" and "Milo" had dozens of other blocks clustered below them, while blocks labeled "Ellen" and "Henry" had only a few.

Gregor clicked on the Jet link and the screen filled with text blocks, some with pictures, others with audio links. Just as Gregor was about to click on one of the groupings of pictures, a system message appeared over Gregor's screen: "HR member access imminent, initiating read-only mode."

"This is not good," Gregor said to himself. He launched a cleanup script, a precaution to help mask his actions. Since most actions on a system made changes to several files simultaneously, Gregor wanted to prevent logging anything on the system he was accessing with any identifiable system information from Gregor's laptop.

Now that Gregor had the background information he needed, it was almost time for execution. Gregor smiled as he manipulated additional Collective Systems databases. Nigel was going to be busy for quite a while.

Gregor launched some custom-made programs to interrogate the database that Viktor and his crew used to schedule fieldwork. They attacked the database administrator's account directly, which gave him full access to the database and everything within. He was able to get past the preliminary database security but encountered an encrypted block that required special handling.

Gregor knew of two people that had access to such privileged information as passwords. Alexei would ask too many questions, but it might be possible to talk Viktor into providing access.

Viktor's phone rang.

"Da?"

"Viktor, I'm running maintenance on the field database and need access to it to clean everything up."

"What do you want me to do about it?"

"Alexei is unreachable, and I need an access password."

"You need my password?"

"Da. I have the database ready."

"Why do you need my password? Why can't you just log in?" Viktor demanded.

Fair question, Gregor thought.

"My backend access isn't working, and I need to get this

maintenance done. There are vulnerabilities on this system. You wouldn't want it to get hacked by outsiders."

"I need to work today. I'm preparing group assignments."

"If you give me your password, I can fix the problems and have you back in within the hour."

"CrazyCats75," Viktor said abruptly. "Capital Cs."

"Is that your password?"

"Da."

Too easy.

With Viktor's password, Gregor was able to unlock the hidden tables. After looking through several pages of field assignments, Gregor noticed a tab labeled "Pending," inside which was a list of names. Gregor didn't know for sure, but he hoped it was a list of targets. Next to each name was lists of known associates and places. Gregor added Nigel Watson's information at the very top of the list, then saved his work.

He notified Viktor that the database was accessible again, then attempted to obfuscate as much about his access as possible.

CHAPTER 16

VIKTOR PUT out his cigarette and lit another.

"He's late!" Viktor bellowed to no one in particular.

It was ten minutes past eight in the morning. Usually Ioann was at least fifteen minutes early! Viktor was just about to call Alexei when Ioann crept up behind him.

"Where have you been?" Viktor demanded.

"I had a problem with transport."

"Are you ready for this?"

"Da."

"Good."

Two hours later, Ioann was perched on top of a building with a view of an alley. Ioann's dossier on Nigel gave details of a picnic table in the alley where the kids usually met, because it was semi-private. Ioann had been watching these kids for a while now; he even left some weatherproof microphones in the vicinity of the picnic table.

Ioann adjusted the scope so he could see the kid's face. He matched the description of the kid that Alexei was looking for. Ioann looked down at his sniper cheat sheet and he identified the kid as Nigel. Shortly after, a tall female with pink hair sat next to Nigel. She had several piercings on her face, most notably her nose. Ioann quickly identified her as Josephine, or Jet, from the dossier. Ioann adjusted his headset to see if his audio connection was working. He heard some ambient noise, but the kids weren't saying much.

The third kid to show was shorter than the two already seated on the picnic table. At first, Ioann could not identify the gender; he moved like a male but appeared to be female. After Ioann made some additional scope adjustments, he finally identified the subject as Milo.

"Do you know where George is?" Milo asked the other two kids.

"Haven't seen him."

Jet nodded in agreement.

Ioann confirmed that Nigel was the head of the little group that Viktor was concerned with. Ioann took aim at Nigel, watched him in the scope for a long moment. Ioann was about to squeeze the trigger and put an end to Nigel when his target suddenly moved.

"Is your Jake problem taken care of?" Jet asked.

"Well sort of. After beating Ralphie up, he not only demanded his money back but he still wanted his character leveled!" Nigel said in disgust.

"Geez, that is rude," Milo interjected.

"I found some code on the Dark Web called Dark Glider. I installed it on Jake's system. I was careful to use a MORP server relay. Also, I'm still trying to help my mother."

Jet gave Nigel a sharp look full of guilt and sad empathy for Ellen.

Milo reached up to pat Nigel on the back, but his sudden movement caused him to slip on some condensation on the picnic table. Milo reached out reflexively and grabbed Nigel's jacket. This entire encounter lasted less than a second but seemed much longer.

Everything else appeared to move in slow motion. Just as Ioann released the trigger, the kid known as Milo suddenly pulled on Nigel's jacket for no apparent reason. The sudden motion caused the bullet to miss its intended target. Instead, it grazed the top left temple of Nigel's head. Nigel suddenly went stiff as blood started dripping down the left side of his head. Then the world went white as he felt real pain for the first time in his short life.

Jet tackled Nigel and both landed hard on broken concrete. Jet felt the wind of something zip past her head.

"Shit," Ioann exclaimed.

Nigel was no longer in view. Ioann was positioning himself to take another shot while Milo screamed at the top of his lungs and ran as fast as his legs would take him. Ioann waited. He had grazed his intended target, but he wasn't visible. He heard a brief surge of panic sirens. Ioann controlled his breathing; he had to maintain control. He would wait until the last possible second before taking his next shot.

Nigel was in extreme pain, and writhed on the ground like a wounded animal. He screamed, whimpered, and cried. Jet kept pressure on the wound.

"Stop wriggling. You need to be still; I have first aid training," Jet yelled in one breath.

Jet knew from her first aid class that she had to keep pressure on open wounds. She pressed with her bare hands. Her mind was racing, trying to take in what had happened.

As Jet continued to put pressure on Nigel's wound, she seemed to relive the previous few seconds. She remembered hearing a distant pop just as Nigel was hit.

Jet didn't know where the shooter—or shooters—may be hiding, so she stayed put, trying to prevent Nigel from bleeding to death. After what seemed like an eternity, she heard sirens.

As the sirens wailed and got louder, Jet's mind drifted. She was suddenly transported back six years. She was in a ballerina outfit. She could hear soft music in the background.

The Nutcracker? she thought. *Yes. Dance of the Sugar Plum Fairy.*

Jet's dance instructor was a harsh woman in her late fifties. Mrs. Anderson? Ms. Davis? She couldn't remember her name. The woman screamed at her again, more urgently. Then, after stumbling for what seemed like the twentieth time, she screamed something unintelligible.

"Josephine! I will not tolerate this disruptive behavior in my class."

As the words trailed off, the woman began screaming in agony. Blood started rolling down the side of her instructor's face.

Jet snapped back into reality.

She tried looking at Nigel, but her vision was obscured by something gooey and sticky. She realized that it was blood, and just as she had this thought, she passed out.

She dreamed she was in Nigel's arms, hearing the lap of ocean waves. They were in a hammock, rocking before a black sand beach. A mist of ocean water sprayed her face. It felt so good. She looked up and saw a strange man speaking Russian. Before she could react, she was pulled from Nigel's arms. Nigel was motionless. She called out to him as blood poured out of several wounds in Nigel's face. Jet screamed.

Jet's first sight when she awoke was a bald, lanky man who was well over six feet tall and dressed in a suit. He was talking with a nurse. Jet felt pain all over, like every nerve ending in her body was stimulated simultaneously.

Jet yelled in agony, then quickly passed out.

Some time later, Jet opened her eyes and saw a woman dressed in light blue scrubs. She tried to say hello, but it came out in a mumble.

Moving her arm was like swimming through a pool of Jell-O. When she tried to move her left arm, she noticed that she was rising, controlling the right arm, spilling over the side of the hospital bed. The nurse rushed over.

"Lie down, Dear," the nurse said.

Jet had no idea that she was trying to sit up. Her actions seemed utterly foreign to her. Simple movements took a lot more effort to produce than Jet thought was possible, and they happened out of sequence. It was as if someone had taken her motor functions and reprogrammed the movements in the wrong order.

"Now, now," the nurse said. "Let's calm down."

"I...am calm," Jet said in a shaky voice.

Jet didn't like the sound of her own voice. It didn't sound like hers at all. All of her confidence had been poured out like a pitcher of water and replaced with something foul. She could smell it, and it sickened her. She closed her eyes again.

When Jet regained consciousness again, she was like a new person. Her left arm felt stiff and a little painful, but moved normally. Her right arm felt better, but she could not move it very far because it was restrained by some sort of harness. She turned her head from side to side. It moved normally, but if she stretched it too far to the left, a sharp pain was present. As she became aware of her surroundings, her mind wandered back to the site of the accident.

"'Accident,' my ass," she said. "That was an assassination attempt!"

As soon as Milo heard gunfire, he ran as fast as he could and didn't look back for a very long time. Milo's skin felt like it was covered in mosquito bites.

Several blocks later, Milo spotted a dumpster that had an open lid. He leapt into it, and the force caused the lid to shift and come down toward his head. Milo ducked, narrowly missing the impact of the very large and heavy lid. His ears were ringing, but he could hear sirens in the distance.

Milo had felt the wind of the bullet fly past his head, narrowly missing him. The exertion from the run caused sweat to get into his eyes, causing more tears. Milo felt something else prick the side of his face as he ran faster.

Milo felt his heart pounding in his chest and pains in his side and arms. *Is this a heart attack?* Dozens of thoughts raced through his head at once, paralyzing him. Milo had a sickening feeling as he dared to hope Nigel and Jet were okay.

He cursed at himself for running away. As far as he knew, his friend was lying on the ground bleeding to death. Jet had jumped on top of Nigel to shield him while Milo ran and hid in this dumpster, like a coward!

The sirens were almost on top of him now. He squirmed in the dark, wet dumpster, trying to get into a comfortable position. In an attempt to conceal himself, Milo was able to move a couple bags over his body. He heard footsteps. He froze.

Is this the shooter? He couldn't tell where the steps were actually coming from; they seemed to be coming from all directions. Milo remained completely still and even held his breath as the footsteps came closer. However, some less-than-stable bags below him began to shift and his body was plunged into the inner side of the dumpster. Milo's heart skipped a beat. The footsteps fell back out of range. He sat very still for a long time.

As he sat in the dark, smelly, dirty dumpster, the wail of sirens continued. He dared not open the dumpster lid.

Milo thought it was unlikely the shooter would have accomplices, but he didn't want to take chances.

He decided it was best to stay put. Then Milo remembered the radio sitting at the bottom of the backpack! Milo immediately started fishing through his backpack. He had to rely on his hands to guide the way. He found it after a minute of intense searching.

Milo was obsessed with radios of all kinds, which is why his civilian volunteer father let him use his handheld scanner.

Milo fiddled with the dials until he heard a rather loud squawk and the radio came to life in his hands, sounding as if several people were talking at once. He managed to find the volume button and lowered it as much as he could.

Ioann wasn't completely sure that Nigel was dead. It looked like he was hit. He didn't expect the smaller kid to jump up and pull Nigel like that! From Ioann's scope, it appeared that Nigel was hit on his temple. As the bullet hit Nigel, the other kids jumped in panic, and the smaller child ran away. Ioann had him in his sights and could have ended him, but hesitated since the only approved target that deserved the hit was the older kid, Nigel.

By the time Ioann changed positions and fired again, Nigel was out of sight. Did he hit the girl by mistake?

He sat in indecision for several seconds which felt like minutes. He needed the kill confirmed.

Ioann was confident that he hadn't been seen; his hiding place was well hidden. However, the rifle was louder than expected. He did so much research when choosing his location but missed one important element: the acoustics of the alley! Even if he used the best suppression silencer, there would have been some noise—the click-click of the gun, the clank of the barrel.

Sweat poured into his eyes as he performed the cleanup process. He wiped each piece of the rifle clean of prints and disassembled the weapon.

When he finished, he calmly walked away from the scene. The rifle set looked like a large duffle bag to the untrained eye. He walked across a board that was placed between two buildings. When he was on the other side, he pulled the board toward him, then placed it gently on the roof. He walked quickly down a fire escape. As he approached one of the dumpsters in the alley, he heard a radio come to life. He also heard a series of sirens coming closer by the second. He lifted the first dumpster lid. It was half full, so he reached in and made room toward the bottom for his duffle bag. He knew it was a matter of time before it was discovered. Better found here than in his possession.

Some time later, Nigel awoke to the chatter of several men, some in plain clothes, others in Milford police uniforms.

"He's awake!" said a large bald man.

"The patient needs his rest. Get out of here," a nurse demanded.

"Your patient is a witness to a crime, and I need to question him."

"Fine, just you."

The room emptied so fast that it alarmed Nigel. He looked around the room.

I'm in the hospital, Nigel said to himself. He reached up reflexively and felt bandages on his head.

The bald man held out his hand.

"I'm Detective Foster. I need to ask you a few questions."

Nigel just nodded. His throat was in a knot.

"Do you know who shot you?" Detective Foster asked.

Nigel opened his mouth but couldn't speak. It all flooded back. If Milo hadn't grabbed him at just that moment, Nigel would be dead.

"What's the matter with him?" Detective Foster asked a nurse.

"He's in shock. I need to get the doctor."

CHAPTER 17

"How are you feeling?"

The first person Nigel saw when he opened his eyes was a tall bald man in a suit. The room was large enough to accommodate two beds. He heard beeping sounds. Something was pulling at his arm; it was tubing that led up to an IV. Nigel could easily see out the window; he had a view of the inlet that led to the ocean. The bed next to his was unoccupied. *I'm in the hospital?*

"Who are you?" Nigel asked the man.

"I'm Detective Foster of the Milford Police Department. I need to ask you a few questions."

"Where are my mother and brother? Where are my friends?"

"Your family is in the waiting room. Your friend, Josephine, is recovering in the room next door."

Nigel just stared into space, taking it all in.

"Do you know why someone would want to harm you or Josephine?"

"I had a third friend with me, Milo."

"We found him hiding in a dumpster several blocks from the incident. He is being questioned now."

"Can I see them?"

"Not until we get this sorted out," Detective Foster said. "Now, please answer my previous question: Do you know who would want to hurt you or your friends?"

"NO!" Nigel shouted.

"Please calm down, Nigel. We cannot leave until this matter is resolved."

Nigel sighed.

The questioning lasted several hours. Detective Foster asked the same questions over and over.

"I will be right back, Nigel. Please stay here."

Nigel winced as he started pulling the tape connecting the IVs to his wrist. The floor was cold to the touch; he started shivering as he made his way across the room to the closet where his clothes were kept. He put on his jacket and shoes. He kept the rest of his clothes in a plastic bag.

He opened the door which led to the hallway, trying to be as quiet as possible. Two uniformed officers were talking about twenty feet from his room.

He walked quickly past the nurses' station, then proceeded left down another hallway. A door blocked his way and wouldn't budge. He scanned the walls for a way to control the door. A large hand grasped his shoulder. Nigel spun his head so fast he felt something pull in his neck.

It was Detective Foster and two uniformed officers.

"Where do you think you're going?"

The uniformed officers escorted him back to his room.

"See to it that his door is manned until all of my questions are answered."

Nigel was interrogated for several more hours before Detective Foster was satisfied.

"Thank you for your cooperation. Your family will be permitted to see you now," Detective Foster said as he left the room.

Permitted to see me? Am I a suspect?

Several minutes later, Ellen and Ralphie appeared.

"Nige!" Ralphie said excitedly as he ran over to him.

Tears were forming in Ellen's eyes. She gasped as she examined Nigel's bandages. The doctor told her that Nigel was lucky; the bullet grazed his temple. Other than some scarring, there would be no permanent damage.

"Are you okay?" Ellen said in a quivering voice.

"I have a headache—probably from all the questioning—but I'm okay. Do you know if I can leave?"

"The doctors want to keep you another night for observation, but I will be back here in the morning."

"You're leaving?"

"Visiting hours have long passed. The doctor said I could see you before I had to leave, but I can't stay over."

Nigel's face flushed as he watched his mother and brother leave. He was angry that his time was cut short by Detective Foster, who offered absolutely no information as to who was trying to shoot them.

Nigel got up and opened his door; there weren't any uniformed cops or anyone else in sight.

He opened the door to the room next to his and saw Jet lying on a bed next to a window. She appeared to be sleeping. Nigel's heart skipped a beat when he noticed her condition. Bandages covered most of her face. Her left arm was in a sling.

"Can I help you?" a female voice said.

Nigel spun around and saw a woman in hospital scrubs. "I'm checking on my friend."

"She's lucky to be alive. She suffered two gunshot wounds. One shattered several bones in her left arm; another grazed her forehead."

Nigel felt paralyzed. All he could do was stare at Jet for a very long time. His eyesight blurred. Nigel felt emptiness inside.

▣

Nigel couldn't sleep. Every time he closed his eyes he saw Jet on top of him—and not in a good way either. His eyes, blurring with blood, distorted Jet's lovely features.

He awoke in a cold sweat. The rays of first morning's light appeared in the room. *The nurse forgot to close the blinds again —no matter.* Nigel loved the sunshine. He observed how the rays came in and reflected on various pieces of equipment in the room, creating wonderful projections on the walls and curtains separating the hospital beds.

Nigel heard some commotion outside his room; it sounded like it was coming from the room next to his. *Is Jet awake?* Nigel carefully jumped out of bed, taking care not to pull the IVs that were held in place by medical tape. Nigel wheeled the unit carrying the IVs into the hallway. He felt a cool breeze across his backside as he made his way to Jet's room.

Jet was eating breakfast from a tray; none of the food looked appetizing to Nigel. *C'mon, who serves Jell-O for breakfast anyway?*

Jet smiled as Nigel made his way over to her bedside. "How are you holding up?"

Jet looked at Nigel's bandages on his head. She was relieved that Nigel retained most of his facial features. During the incident, Nigel's face was covered in blood, and it was diffi-cult to determine how many wounds he had.

"I've been a whole lot better." Nigel winced as she attempted to eat the Jell-O with a spoon in her good hand.

"I'm left-handed. I'm not sure if you knew."

Nigel shook his head.

"Which makes it almost impossible to eat."

Nigel shifted his IV unit around to her right side. He took her spoon and fed her using slow and deliberate motions.

"I'm being released today," Jet said.

"Wow, that was quick."

"Doctors treated my injuries as best as they can. My mother is supposed to pick me up any minute now. The nurse wants to make sure I eat everything first. Do you want something from my tray?"

Nigel's nose crinkled. "No thanks."

Jet laughed.

"We should discuss the attempt on our lives. I want to compare notes. Something is very wrong here," Nigel said.

Jet gave Nigel a concerned look. "I'm not sure I'm ready to talk about it. I mean, I do...I just need more time."

Nigel nodded. "I understand. Let's plan to meet soon."

"If I can," Jet said.

What does that mean?

Before Nigel could process that thought, he was interrupted.

"Mr. Watson! I need for you to return to your room. Josephine's mother is waiting at the nurses' station. She doesn't want to see a half-naked teenager."

Nigel flushed.

Jet gigged.

"Pick this up later?" Nigel asked.

Jet nodded and gave him a smile.

Milo tossed his radio frequency scanner into his backpack. As he entered the alley where the incident happened, he froze as he relived the experience of being chased. Police tape was strewn around the alley haphazardly. Milo wondered if they even finished processing the crime scene.

He began scanning for anything with a radio frequency. He had had the feeling that they were being watched that day but failed to act. He felt guilty for not at least saying anything. Jet and Nigel probably would have dismissed the feelings anyway. Milford was a small town, and nothing like this had ever happened—in his lifetime anyway. The frequency scanner would emit a loud, high-pitched tone if the scanner came too close to a device that had a frequency.

Milo didn't find anything for a long time; he was about to give up when he heard a slightly higher tone than usual. The difference was subtle but there. The picnic table was clean. Milo confirmed by physically checking it. Judging from the signal strength, Milo determined another signal was being transmitted from another location nearby, within thirty feet. Other than some scattered debris, there was little else an intruder could bug. *Perhaps the assassin had a powerful directional microphone?*

Frustrated, Milo leaned against a wooden fence separating the alley from the back ends of other businesses. His scanner screeched to life. He jumped at the abrupt sound. Milo examined the fence; although he could not see anything, his scanner told a different story. He moved the probe methodically across the fence until he found what he was looking for. He examined the probed area in more detail and noticed an imperfection in the wood. Someone went through a lot of trouble to conceal whatever this was. He took out his Swiss Army knife and poked at the edges. Something dislodged. A pill-looking thing was attached to a stiff wire. He tugged on the wire and felt it pull. He also heard something fall. *From the other side?*

Milo scaled the fence and saw what he was looking for: A small box was attached to the wire. He jumped to the other side, detached the wire, and shoved the box and the wire into his backpack. He wanted to investigate at a safe location because he didn't know who else might be watching.

After the attack, Nigel wanted to ensure secure communication with his friends, since their previous communications via the game were breached somehow. Nigel smiled at the idea of communication via a mobile app.

Milford was a small town, but not so small that it didn't have a local computer shop. Mr. Henry, who ran Better Buy Computers, spent a lot of time with his customers, a move that set his shop apart from the big guys. He held free seminars and classes, teaching local townsfolk anything from spreadsheets to internet access.

It was even rumored that Mr. Henry was a former government agent. If anyone knew how to protect communications, it was Mr. Henry!

The day he got out of the hospital, Nigel walked into Better Buy Computers. Mr. Henry was helping an elderly woman with her tablet.

"Be right with you, Nige."

Nigel thanked him as he browsed the display cases. Approximately ten minutes later, Mr. Henry called out for Nigel. As Nigel approached, he involuntarily looked around the store for any threat that may have been lurking.

"Can we talk in private?" Nigel asked.

"Sure. It's time for my lunch break anyway."

Mr. Henry turned over the "Be Back Soon" sign and locked the front door. Nigel followed him toward the back of the store. The hallway narrowed to reveal a room just big enough to fit a desk and a couple of chairs.

"Have a seat, Nigel."

Nigel sat in the small guest chair.

"How can I help you?"

"Mr. Henry, if I wanted to send a message securely without having to rely on email client encryption, how would I do it?"

"Why are you so interested?"

"A school project, just doing research. As part of the project, I need to interview an expert on the subject and submit a written report along with a prototype."

"Oh! Well, email is the most common method, but you do have a couple other options. You could use a mobile encryption service that actually uses its own network. While it's secure, the only one I know of is run by a company in Russia."

"What if I wanted to send messages through cryptocurrency networks?" Nigel asked.

"Before I answer that, how much do you know about cryptocurrencies?"

"I know they are a new form of digital money, but that is about it."

"Correct. Some of the secure coins offer messaging services, but there is a catch," Mr. Henry explained. "Cryptocurrency networks charge a small fee for the service. The downside is that everyone on the recipient list must have a 'wallet.' This wallet not only stores the cryptocurrency, but the messages as well."

"Right, each recipient of the secure message I send will need their own address and wallet to send messages to. Any other downsides?"

"Transactions, including secure messages, take time to

process. Remember that the transactions need to be verified a number of times before the cryptocurrency can be transferred, and the same is true for a message."

"Would you be willing to help me put something together?"

"Absolutely!"

Agent Appleton did his daily search on Collective activity and found some pattern matches showing up when certain encryption activity was present on publicly routable networks. Agent Appleton was shocked when he noticed all coordinates of the matches were strangely concentrated in and around Milford, that town where he helped that woman who got hacked a couple weeks ago.

This couldn't be a coincidence.

Helping Ellen Watson wasn't Agent Appleton's primary goal—finding what possible network activity that placed a member of The Collective behind her keyboard was. Agent Appleton needed to know what technical information could possibly be in the logs that were gathered by the FBI forensics team. The only problem was that team was already overcommitted and equally overworked. He needed to find a technically capable person that would keep a secret. Maybe that Henry fellow...assuming he wasn't a Collective spy.

CHAPTER 18

THE MORE MILO thought about the encounter, the less it made sense.

Was the alley bugged? Were they being watched from above? Milo pondered these questions as he called Nigel.

"How are you feeling?" Milo asked as soon as Nigel answered.

"I feel sore all over. I'm also pissed and confused."

"Did the police say if they had any suspects?" Milo asked.

"No. They're completely useless. This detective interrogated me for hours before I could even see my family. As if *I* was the bad guy!"

"Have you seen Jet or George since you got home?"

"They haven't returned my calls or texts, but I'll keep trying."

"I can't get what happened out of my mind. I thought both of you were dead."

"If Jet hadn't tackled me, I would be," Nigel said bitterly.

"I think that we were being stalked from above. There are a few tall buildings close to our meeting spot," Milo said.

"Someone had to know we would be there. The only communication we used was in *The Colossal Machine*. Obviously someone hacked the game, or else one of our phones," Nigel said. "But I have an alternate communications solution. Mr. Henry from Better Buy is going to help us."

Milo picked up his phone. It was Nigel.

"That is strange. I was just thinking I should give you a call and you rang."

"I just sent you a text. Please tap on the link to install it."

Milo did as Nigel asked.

"A cryptocurrency app?"

"It is a Digibit communications app that I wrote. It will allow you to send covert messages through the Digibit network."

"Wow, I didn't know that was possible."

"Normally it isn't, but Mr. Henry knows a lot about encryption, and between my programming and his skills, I was able to develop an app."

"Awesome! How does it work?"

"First, I will need to send you some Digibit crypto. Once you have that, it costs a small fraction to send a message through its secure application programming interface, or API."

"Are our phones safe?"

"I'm not sure if the Pretzelverse communication app installed any malicious code; I haven't been able to find any, but I don't want to take that chance."

Several minutes later, they were talking over a secure Digibit link. The communication wasn't instant, but at least Nigel was positive that it wasn't being tapped.

"Jet contacted me. She wants to meet," Nigel said via the Digitbit link.

"When and where?"

"At the computer lab after school tomorrow."

"I don't have access to that lab yet. But I think I know a way in."

"Okay, in the back of the lab there is a break room that students can reserve for collaborations. I have made a reservation."

"See you tomorrow, Nige."

Milo had to work quickly if he wanted to enter the school's computer lab undetected tomorrow. He took a large binder that contained his plans from a shelf and took out the plans for the radio frequency cloner. Milo subscribed to several hobbyist websites that contained radio frequency schematics. He scanned the parts list. He had most of the parts, but he needed more. Since Milford didn't contain an electronics store, he had to improvise. He scavenged the part from his scanner. A few hours later, he had a radio frequency (RF) cloner.

Milo's third-period class was close to the computer lab, and all he had to do was wait outside the door of his class while the kids entering the computer lab used their access cards. *I will see how simple this really is,* Milo thought.

The next morning, he almost failed before he could even scan a single card. A large oaf of a boy slammed into him just before his third period.

"Move, Slow Poke," a voice called out. It was Jake.

Jake slammed into Milo with enough force to make his project inoperable. Milo went to the restroom and made some quick field repairs, then was only able to capture a few RF signals before he had to get to class. He needed to work through lunch if his plan had any chance of success.

As soon as the lunch bell rang, Milo headed to the school

library, where he could work on his project undisturbed. It took some time to verify and transfer the clone card data and imprint a new card. He placed the imprinted card just behind his school ID so it would go unnoticed until he needed it.

Nigel got to the computer lab early enough so he could work out what he wanted to say to Jet. About twenty minutes later, Jet entered with a grimace. She was sweating from the exertion of the effort it took to come to the computer lab. Nigel hadn't seen her in any of their shared classes. *Did she make a special trip?*

Nigel hurried to the door to help her. She made a go-away gesture.

"Let me help; you're in pain."

"Sorry, I want to try it myself. No one at home will let me do anything. Even George has been helping."

"I didn't see you at school today, or even this week so far."

"Your wounds can be concealed..." Jet trailed off, lost in thought.

Nigel gave Jet a light hug, not wanting to cause any more pain than necessary.

After the embrace, he noticed that Jet was on the verge of tears.

"Have a seat," Nigel said, pulling a chair out.

"I'm surprised you wanted to meet at school of all places."

"Right now, it is one of the few places I feel safe."

Nigel didn't say anything for a long time. He frowned and pressed a finger around the bandages.

"How are you holding up?" Jet asked. "You seem to be in pain as well."

"It's fine. The doctor said the bullet grazed my scalp. It hurts like hell at times, but eventually it goes away."

"My dad's coming home early from a long-term assignment."

Does she not want her father to come home?

"In fact, I cannot stay long. My mother wants me to be home when my father returns."

"I was going to wait for Milo to show up, but I think we need to talk about the incident. Do you have any clue as to why we would be targets? Does it have anything to do with the Dark Web?" Nigel asked.

"I can't see why. Everything we did was anonymous. Have you explored the Dark Web on your own?"

Dark Glider, but I was careful. "I downloaded a *Colossal Machine* automation tool. I was careful."

"Careful or not, someone wanted you dead," Jet said.

Nigel looked down.

"I'm sorry, I didn't mean for it to come out that way."

"Which way?" asked Milo.

Nigel didn't hear him come in. Jet looked surprised, too.

"We were just going over what happened."

"Oh."

"Do you even have access to the computer lab, Milo?" Jet asked.

"Well—technically, no, but I was able to clone an ID that helped me enter the lab."

Nigel smiled; his friends always found a way to help.

"We were trying to figure out how the killer may have found out about Nigel," Jet said. "It wasn't a random shooting; it was targeted."

Milo seemed lost in thought, then finally spoke. "When I heard shots, I ran and hid in a dumpster." He looked ashamed.

"Go on," said Nigel.

"From inside the dumpster, I heard footsteps come and go. When I thought it was safe, I turned on my dad's radio that I was going to show you guys."

Milo swallowed. Nigel could see his Adam's apple move in his throat.

Nobody said anything for a long time.

"The voices I heard had accents," Milo said. "I can't place them, but it could be Eastern European. I'm not sure. I did hear some names."

Milo thought some more before continuing.

"I heard names like Viktor, Owen, I think, Alexei, and Greg or Gregor. I also heard something about a Collective. Any of those names mean anything to either of you?"

Jet shook her head.

"I think I know. After my mom was hacked, I applied for a job to make ends meet." Nigel flushed, licked his lips, and fidgeted in his seat.

It wasn't easy, but Jet put her good hand on one of Nigel's hands. After a few minutes, he regained his composure.

"A few weeks before the incident, I was invited to a weekend retreat at Eldon Tage's mansion."

"And you just now mention it!" Milo exclaimed. "It is Eldon Tage we are talking about? He is the largest employer in Milford. My dad works for him."

Nigel looked at Jet. She was stone-faced.

"I was going to tell you, but it must have slipped my mind."

Nigel relayed most of the events from the weekend as well as some of his assignments. He felt it was wise to leave out the intimate details concerning his encounter with Natasha.

"Is it possible that someone from the event would want to harm you?" Milo asked.

"I kept getting programming assignments that had misinformation or errors. I corrected them when I submitted the assignments. I actually got a personal thank-you from Alexei Breven himself."

"Who?" Milo asked.

"Mr. Breven is the CEO and Founder of Collective Systems, Inc."

"What does that tell you, Nige?" Jet questioned.

Nigel's eyes widened as he thought about the implications.

"Is there someone you trust—I mean really trust—inside Collective Systems?" Jet prodded him further.

Nigel thought for a moment.

"Natasha always has my back."

Ioann received an urgent message on his burner phone: "Call dispatch!"

From the inside coat pocket, he pulled out a pair of glasses and a woolen flat cap. After several minutes, he took out the flip-phone and held down the number two button. The words "Joe's Plumbing" were briefly displayed on the device.

After the second ring, someone picked up.

"Joe's Plumbing, dispatch speaking."

"I have an emergency situation. My upstairs pipes are leaking," Ioann said in a perfect American accent.

"What is your location?"

"In an upstairs apartment near the water."

"I can have someone there very soon."

Rocco's phone rang just after picking up his oldest child Louie from soccer practice. His dash read, "Joe's Plumbing."

He thought they would never call again. How long had it

been? Two, three, four months? That didn't matter now. Rocco tapped the ear icon on the phone control panel so his son couldn't eavesdrop.

"Your services are required, Mr. Surelli."

"Who is this?" Rocco asked.

"Dispatch," the voice said. "You have twenty seconds to accept. I need a verbal answer."

"Affirmative," Rocco said.

"I will text you the details in Sandbox now. You need to respond within ten minutes."

Without missing a beat, Rocco pulled over to the side of the highway. Rocco pulled out the burner smartphone he kept in his coat's inside pocket, tapped in the code, verified facial and thumb biometrics, then pulled up the app called Sandbox.

The icon for this app looked like any normal game. It even had a splash screen that briefly showed a happy shovel and several bugs playing around the shovel. One of the bugs looked like a mean centipede. If it were real, it would surely sting Rocco. It was irrational, but Rocco got nervous just looking at that splash screen.

The main interface for Sandbox was visible now, and after a few taps, Rocco was at the message section. He tapped the message, and a thirty-second timer started counting backward.

Great, lots of words! Rocco thought.

Rocco was good at memorizing addresses, especially around Milford. He immediately recognized 3358 Lighthouse Drive. That was in the center of town. He tapped the accept button with just two seconds to spare.

Rocco was currently on the north side of the inlet that led into town. It was easily a ten-minute drive.

"Louie, I have a work emergency. Are you cool with hanging out at the coffee shop?"

"Whatever, Dad."

"Thanks, Son. I will pick you up soon."

Rocco pulled up at the Coffee Barn and handed Louie a twenty. Rocco drove another three blocks south, then parked the car in an unmarked spot off the main road.

Two minutes later, Rocco opened the door at the top suite at 3358 Lighthouse Drive and saw Ioann waiting for him.

"Joe's Plumbing!"

"If the wind is brisk and the shade is dark, where do I go?"

"Icelandia," Rocco said as he tossed Ioann the keys to his vehicle. Ioann nodded, then left. After a few minutes, Rocco left the scene.

Agent Appleton reviewed Janice's dossier, which contained a rather old picture of William Stohl. Agent Appleton reviewed it again before leaving his vehicle and entering the store.

"Greetings, welcome to Better Buy Computers."

"Is Mr. Henry here?"

"I'm Mr. Henry," answered the clerk.

Agent Appleton examined the clerk closely. He seemed way too young to be Stohl.

"Is Mr. Henry Senior here?"

"My dad's at home, working on his retirement. I run the store five days a week."

"When is he expected back?"

"He called in sick today, so no telling. What is this about anyway?"

"I'm an old friend."

"Really? Where did you meet him?"

"Friends at the Bureau," Agent Appleton said.

"Okay, I will tell him you came by. What is your name again?"

Agent Appleton handed the clerk an envelope. "Just see that he gets this."

Mr. Henry Junior entered his parents' farmhouse. It had been a couple of years since Mr. Henry Junior had been here, and the pain was still fresh. *I miss you, Mom,* Mr. Henry Junior thought.

"Back here, Son."

Mr. Henry Junior entered his father's study. Mr. Henry Senior enjoyed his privacy, and his study afforded certain protections.

"A man came looking for you today. He said you were friends at the Bureau. He also gave me this."

Mr. Henry Junior handed the envelope to his father. Mr. Henry Senior opened it and read the handwritten note.

"I know that you are not who you say you are. Call for details."

"Thank you for bringing this to my attention, Son."

Mr. Henry Junior knew that tone of voice well. He gave his father some privacy.

Agent Appleton's card was attached to the letter. Mr. Henry Senior called the number listed on the card.

"I don't know who you are, but leave my family out of it," he said.

"I think we need to meet."

A loud rapping noise came from the front of the farmhouse. Mr. Henry answered the door.

"Agent Appleton, FBI. May I come in?"

Agent Appleton held out his Bureau credentials. Mr. Henry led Agent Appleton to his study.

"What do you want?"

Agent Appleton produced a copy of the memorandum that Brennen and Stohl wrote so many years ago. Mr. Henry just looked at the paper in disbelief.

"I need help identifying some malicious actors. This paper suggests that I can identify programmers by code signature. The problem is that I don't understand the technical aspects of this process."

"Why don't you ask the authors?"

"The lead author is dead, but the co-author is standing before me. Isn't that right, Mr. Stohl?"

Mr. Henry's expression immediately changed. "Agent Stohl is also dead. I think you need to go."

"I don't think you understand what is at stake here. The Bureau is overwhelmed with evidence of hacking attempts throughout the country. It's not just the large corporations either; there are lots of victims at small banks getting robbed. Even here in Milford."

"I don't understand why you need my help when you have the entire Bureau at your disposal."

"I need the help of someone that can track an IP address to a physical location, which takes the Bureau days. I need a person who can get me a resource, or point me to software I don't understand when I need it."

"In my day, everyone knew how to do basic technical tasks, like finding an IP," Mr. Henry said with a sigh. "Come by the computer shop tomorrow and I will help you. Now please leave."

Agent Appleton left without another word.

Alexei scanned the latest Collective intelligence reports. He didn't like what he was reading.

"Scans and communications with known FBI servers?"

"Da," Viktor said.

"How is this possible? Key members of The Collective's board of directors will be summoned," Alexei said. "Given the travel requirements alone, it will be a minimum of forty-eight hours before we get everyone together in person. We need to have a meeting. I will authorize a hosted teleconference over a secure connection. Communicate the time for 6 a.m. UTC Friday morning. I know it's less than twelve hours' notice, but this is an emergency. Notify dispatch!"

Gregor was perched in his favorite hidden enclave. From his vantage point, he could see several tourists below enjoying an espresso at a patio café. The café was a favorite because it had absolutely no security on its Wi-Fi network. It also used 802.11b radio technology, which allowed Gregor's antenna to boost his signal.

Once Gregor's impostor signal captured some unsuspecting machines, a lot of network data could be decrypted almost as fast as Gregor could read it.

Gregor was about to hit the exploit button when he received an urgent call from dispatch.

"If the sky is white, what is devoid at the end of khan?"

"Rainbow," Gregor said.

"What is the primary key?"

"16-11-52."

"Identity confirmed. Hold for dispatch."

After a few clicks, Gregor was greeted by another voice that sounded far away.

"What is your C-ID?" the dispatcher asked.

"2341."

"Operative Gobechov, you have a message. Would you like to hear it now?"

"Da."

"Acknowledged. Hold for message."

A prerecorded message played in Russian.

"Greetings, Comrade. If you are listening to this message, an emergency meeting of The Collective has been called by the chief architect. The meeting will occur at 6 a.m. UTC on the morrow. It is of the utmost importance that you attend. Additional instructions will be sent just before the meeting."

The message abruptly stopped. Gregor ended the call and immediately destroyed the burner phone by breaking it in half and destroying the SIM chip.

CHAPTER 19

"OKAY. If I agree to help, then I want something in return," Mr. Henry said.

"Name it," Agent Appleton said.

"A favor of my choosing."

"We have a deal, Mr. Henry. You have my word! Before we start, I need to read you in."

Agent Appleton produced a small tablet from his pocket and handed it to Mr. Henry for signature confirmation. After a few swipes and taps, Mr. Henry handed the tablet back to Agent Appleton.

"Show me what you have."

Agent Appleton opened his briefcase and took out a small laptop. On the screen appeared to be a group of ciphertext.

"At first, we thought it was a standard algorithm, like SHA-512 or AES-256, but none of the agents that I know have ever seen this," Agent Appleton said.

"Can you give me a copy?"

Agent Appleton copied the file on a spare flash drive and handed it to Mr. Henry. Mr. Henry uploaded the file to his decryption workstation.

"In recent years, I have developed code to allow the decryption of a file or a piece of ciphertext in a distributed manner," Mr. Henry explained. "In other words, I can use many computers all around the world to help with the process."

"How many computers do you have?"

"About fourteen servers here in Milford, another ten in data centers in Los Angeles and New York, and another hundred elsewhere I can spin up on demand."

Agent Appleton looked shocked. "I had no idea that this could be done. I mean, privately."

"Parallel processing hasn't been fully realized by individuals until recently," Mr. Henry explained.

The file was less than 1 percent decrypted. Mr. Henry frowned.

"Now I will introduce the remaining twenty-three servers to aid in the decryption process."

Mr. Henry typed rapidly.

"There! Let's see how long this takes. My decryption program is like piecing together a puzzle; I have sent the output of the decrypted file in progress to another monitor."

Mr. Henry pointed to large screen on the other side of his office, on which zeros and ones appeared.

"Looks like computer gibberish."

"Ahh, but it's not. Let me translate."

Mr. Henry pulled out a blank sheet of paper and began writing furiously. He wrote "192.168.1.0" and handed it to Agent Appleton.

"Do you understand how transport layer security works?" Mr. Henry asked.

"I don't. That is why I need your help."

"In layman's terms, each computer that participates on a network needs an IP address, which can either be 32- or 128-bit. The most common is an IPv4 address, which is usually a series of numbers like this with periods between them. I'm sure you've seen them before." He pointed to the paper. "We can trace the IP address back to a physical address, as well. Do you have a suspected IP address?"

After a moment, Agent Appleton recited the IP address of 32.210.193.52 from his notes. Mr. Henry brought up an IP locator tool.

After a few more clicks, Mr. Henry was able to give Agent Appleton the address to 302 Sycamore Lane, Milford.

"Consider this an address of interest," Mr. Henry said. "What else do you need help with?"

"I need to understand how these code patterns work. How can I find out who wrote a particular piece of code?"

"Wait here."

Mr. Henry left the office for several minutes, then returned with a red USB flash drive.

"I've developed a scanner that will identify these unique patterns, but doing the leg work is up to you."

Mr. Henry provided a brief demonstration of how his program worked, then handed it to Agent Appleton.

Gregor wasn't satisfied with the progress the FBI had made in apprehending Nigel, so he decided to make things a little more interesting. After the usual precautions were taken, Gregor navigated the Dark Web for a forum called the Black Iris. The site was popular, not because it was a gambling site, but because it was an online bounty board. Gregor clicked on the link and was directed to a blank page.

"Damn, why isn't it working?" Gregor yelled.

This outburst woke Dunya, who had fallen asleep on the couch in Gregor's apartment. She stumbled in the general direction of the bedroom. Gregor found his mind drifting to the pleasant memory of a night of dancing, booze, and...*other things.*

Gregor scolded himself for his brief distraction. He really needed to find the Black Iris.

After a lot of searching on various Dark Web sites, Gregor had an epiphany. The location of the site was seasonal. Black Iris site administration was paranoid of a site takedown. The solution involved granting premium members with a way to easily learn the site location.

Gregor had been given a small rectangular piece of equipment with a fingerprint reader; he quickly located it and launched the program. He was greeted with a black screen with a single sentence that read, "Place finger in correct position." A series of numbers that counted down from twenty appeared. After two attempts, Gregor was able to unlock the updated URL and access information. The procedure was nerve wracking because after three attempts the device would deactivate.

A few minutes later, he carefully typed in the random string of letters and numbers that allowed site access. Although it had been a long time since Gregor accessed the site, he remembered the gray-on-black image of an iris. Underneath the iris was a vine made of barbed wire. "There it is," Gregor said as he clicked on the "Submit Bounty" link.

The page was a standard form that asked several questions about the bounty that was to be placed: name or online persona and last known physical statistics, such as appearance, address, known haunts, associates, and other information that could help with a positive match.

The Required Proof section of the page was particularly interesting to Gregor because a number of non-standard options were available. For instance, the standard option was a photo or video upload. However, for an additional fee, other more interesting options were made available—such as dismemberment or "souvenirs." Gregor dismissed it all. He was on a strict timetable. A standard approach was better suited for his needs.

Gregor knew almost everything about Nigel: his full name, address, school, online activity. He also had detailed information on all of his known associates. Once he was satisfied, he clicked on the submit button. A Digibit wallet address appeared with the amount of 5.516DB. Additional payments would be required upon the acceptance of a suitable bounty hunter. Gregor immediately sent the payment and shut down the connection.

Since the attempt on his life, Nigel had been on edge. He often felt like he was being watched, especially when alone, or at night. His work for Collective Systems and his character-leveling business both came to a halt.

Nigel was considering going to a doctor when he looked at his phone. Ten messages. Two from Milo, three from Jake, one from his mother, four from Collective Systems, and one last message from Jet. Nigel immediately opened Jet's.

"Dear Nigel, sorry that I have been out of touch this past week. It breaks my heart to tell you this, but my parents have decided to move out of the area. My father has insisted that I don't associate with my friends in Milford until the psycho that tried to kill us is captured. I hope we will be able to see each other again soon, but for the time being it is not possible. You will always be in my heart. Yours truly, Jet."

Nigel couldn't swallow for several seconds.

Her parents took her away! he thought. *I'm going to find who did this, even if the cops can't!*

It took Nigel a long time before he checked his other messages. He opened the message from Milo.

"Hey, Nige! How are you feeling? Hear from Jet? Give me a call if you want to talk."

The message from Jake was less menacing than he would have thought.

"Hey, Nigel, just wanted to see how you were doing. I haven't seen you around school, and I just learned what happened. Don't worry about leveling the characters to max, just give me what you have. No hurry though. BTW...How are you feeling?"

Nigel was astonished by Jake's message. He was expecting more threats.

I will take all the good luck I can get, Nigel thought.

Nigel opened the messages from Collective Systems. Three were job offers. The fourth was from Natasha.

"Nigel, I'm concerned that you haven't accepted a task in over a week. Is there a problem I can help you with? Please call me. It is imperative that I speak with you."

After two days of twenty-four computers utilizing hundreds of core processors, Mr. Henry received an alert that the decryption process was completed.

Mr. Henry underestimated how long it would take to decode the blob of ciphertext that Agent Appleton gave him. The size of the file wasn't very large, but its encryption algorithm was based on SHA-256, an older but effective form of encryption.

The payload consisted of a folder archive with some source

code and some sort of log. Mr. Henry proceeded to run it through his analysis program. The output suggested that multiple people contributed to the code.

Mr. Henry called Agent Appleton.

"I think you need to get over here right away."

"What did you find?"

"Several things, but I'd rather not talk on the phone."

"I can be there in the late afternoon."

"Get here as soon as you can!"

As Nigel was checking messages, Natasha called.

"Hello?"

"Nigel!"

"Sorry I haven't been in touch. I had a...family emergency to deal with."

"I hope it's not something serious?"

Nigel couldn't answer.

"Nigel, you there?"

"Yes," he said, sobbing.

"I think we need to meet up. I'm about an hour from your location."

"Okay."

Nigel was too choked up to say much of anything. The doctors at the hospital encouraged him to talk about his feelings with a psychiatrist, but he didn't feel comfortable talking to strangers about his recent experiences. He needed a friend now more than ever.

About forty-five minutes later, Natasha knocked on Nigel's front door.

"I think we should talk in the car."

Nigel followed Natasha to a large sedan with tinted

windows. Rocky was standing near the rear of the car with the door open.

"You haven't acknowledged any of your assignments or communicated with us in almost a week. I thought something might have happened to you!" Natasha said.

"My friends and I nearly died."

"Was there an accident?"

"Someone tried to kill us."

"What? How?"

"Someone attempted to shoot us. My friend Milo pulled me out of the way just in time, then my friend Jet threw herself on me to get me out of the gunfire. I still can't believe she did that. Violence is so rare in Milford. A detective grilled me for hours. I was treated like a suspect; it was awful."

Natasha said nothing for a long time.

"So the shooter is still at large?"

"Yes. The police said they have some leads, but I haven't heard anything in several days."

"Take as much time as you need. There is no hurry to return to work; your place in the program is secure."

"Thank you, but I think I want to return to work as soon as possible. I need to get my mind off it."

"Take it easy, Nigel. Our primary concern is your safety."

"It's not like the work involves leaving the house. I will be fine."

Nigel didn't really believe that, but he thought he sold it to Natasha. He needed the resources of Collective Systems for his private investigation.

CHAPTER 20

ALEXEI POURED A GLASS OF WINE, then opened his nearly indestructible, military-grade laptop. His lifestyle warranted a more durable computer, since he was constantly breaking them. The thing was heavy and unattractive, but didn't get destroyed in remote areas of the world. It also featured a built-in wireless interface and satellite phone attachment.

Currently, he was in a villa off the coast of the Mediterranean. He had a breathtaking view of the moonlight dancing above the sea. Alexei loved the evenings here almost as much as the daylight hours. He loved how the moonlight reflected against the smooth domes and curves of the most unusual villa in which he was currently staying.

The villa was more of a compound than a single residence. Situated on top of a cliff, it was accessible only from a private road leading off a dead end or by helicopter. The helipad was connected to another estate a quarter of a mile down the coast but was accessible via tunnels that were hand carved out of the rock. The previous owner had created the entrance to maintain his privacy. Farther down, past the helipad, was a path that led to a boat dock.

To carve the rock, the previous owner had hired an army of

WHITE HAT BLACK HEART / 185

laborers, masons, and craftsmen to create a tunnel that led to an existing cavern that was below the property. He also had several geologists on staff during the time of the villa's construction. He wanted to ensure that his privacy and security were maintained. The outcome worked well for Alexei.

The only problem with this location was it had significant connectivity issues. While it may have been fine for the corporate executives of the 1970s or '80s, it posed several challenges for the CEO of a modern technology company. He was obsessed with reactions and hated to miss out on the video aspect of a conference call.

As Alexei was contemplating, his red phone rang.

"Da?"

"Are you alone, Darling?" Natasha asked.

"I'm alone."

"We need to talk. I have news I suspect you need confirmation of."

"Can you call me on the secure video uplink?"

"Why?"

"Need to see if the connection is suitable for tomorrow's meeting."

The video connection with Natasha was a disaster. High latency made it impossible, even with audio-only capabilities.

Alexei massaged his temples as he thought about an alternative location. He picked up the phone and called Viktor.

"Privyet, Alexei. What can I do for you?"

"I need a new location with a sufficient internet connection for the meeting. It needs to be in the same city as the chateau."

"I'm on it. I will have a new location within the hour."

Alexei called Natasha back.

"Well, that was painful," Natasha said.

"Indeed. Viktor is working on the technical problems as we speak. What's so urgent?"

"I met with our star intern this afternoon."

Natasha relayed the entire conversation she had with Nigel. Alexei said nothing for a long time.

"You have just confirmed my suspicions," Alexei said with disgust. "There have been only two interns that I have ever sponsored who have shown so much promise. Nigel is one of them. I believe you can guess the second student's identity."

"It breaks my heart. But yes."

Alexei hung up the phone and continued to stare out the circular window in his office.

"What was so secretive that you couldn't give me any details over the phone?" Agent Appleton demanded.

"I believe I have found a Milford connection to The Collective," Mr. Henry said.

"Go on."

"After decrypting the bit of ciphertext that you provided, the payload was a standard archived file," Mr. Henry explained. "The files in the payload appeared to be random until I realized the magic numbers didn't match the file types that I was seeing."

"Magic number?"

"Oh, sorry. When I get excited, I get technical. Several images appeared in the archived file. They appeared to be random images at first, but the size of the disk seemed wrong. I checked the header, and it had the file signature of a memory capture file. I loaded the capture file into my memory analyzer program and was able to extract information out of it. Pieces of a conversation."

"Did it list any specifics? Like names, codenames?"

"Dispatch, Rocky, and Ioann. The IP address originated

from a mobile phone from the Milford area. The capture was too small to piece together more, but I'm able to give you enough information to work with the local cell provider to get additional information."

"You're brilliant!" Agent Appleton said.

Agent Appleton handed Mr. Henry another flash drive.

"The first fragment was a test. The remainder of the evidence should be on here."

"I'll get to work."

Viktor found a nearby chateau with enough bandwidth to support a high-quality video conference. It was a short distance away and accessible via the catacombs between the chateau and the villa.

"Why do we need a high-definition video connection?" Viktor asked.

Alexei liked to view the expressions of people he was questioning. It often gave him clues as to if they were lying.

"To gain a better view of the team," Alexei said. "Is it ready?"

"Da."

Alexei started his end of the video conference and could see video feeds of everyone.

"Thank you for attending this emergency meeting of the principal members of The Collective. It is with a heavy heart that I bring to you the main order of business. It is rare that any member of The Collective fails, but we did fail to eliminate a target on the priority list."

Alexei paused for emphasis.

"A hit was authorized that led Ioann, one of our elite operatives, to eliminate one of our own employees."

Most members of The Collective had looks of utter shock. Alexei looked hard at each member for clues. All but Gregor had subtle signs of anger or contempt. Gregor's reaction was indifference.

Those boys could have done great things together, Alexei thought.

"How did you learn of this treachery, Comrade?" Gregor asked.

"During our latest talent search, we found several promising young and talented penetration testers and machine learning enthusiasts."

Alexei waited to see if any of what he said triggered a response. Gregor was unmoved.

"During a weekend session," Alexei went on, "the interns developed a system to track certain unauthorized movements through the network. They utilized network flow data to capture this activity. After several days, we put together a model, and it pointed to a suspect with 99 percent accuracy."

Finally, a response, Alexei thought when he saw Gregor flinch. *Is that fear?*

"With the help of outside experts, Viktor is in the process of verifying the findings. Soon we will find the betrayer and prove that technology can be effectively used on human behavior based on real evidence," Alexei said excitedly.

Gregor couldn't believe his ears. Alexei trusted that tech to a bunch of interns?

Thanks to Mr. Henry, Agent Appleton was closer to The Collective than ever before. The clues found in the encrypted blob had led him to a vehicle owned by a local man named Rocco "Rocky" Surelli.

"Hello, Mr. Surelli. May I have a word?"

Rocky turned around to see a tall man in a suit holding an FBI badge.

"I have nothing to say," Rocky said.

Agent Appleton produced a piece of paper and handed it to Rocky.

"Let's do it the hard way, then. This is a warrant that gives me legal authority to search your vehicle, phone, and anything else in your possession."

Two Milford Police Department cruisers appeared right on cue, blocking Rocky's car in.

"Surrender your phone, please."

Rocky handed his phone to Agent Appleton. It was locked.

"Unlock it, please."

"No. I know my rights."

"'Hard way,' indeed," Agent Appleton said. He waved the warrant in front of Rocky. "Okay, let's talk about this downtown. This piece of paper also gives me the right to arrest your ass."

Rocky fought as two Milford police officers took him into custody.

Unlike his phone, Mr. Surelli's car was unlocked. During a search of the vehicle, Agent Appleton found and seized a laptop. Since it normally took days, if not weeks, to get a laptop analyzed by the FBI, Agent Appleton decided to enlist Mr. Henry's help again.

Several hours later, Mr. Henry returned the laptop and a signed chain of custody form back to Agent Appleton.

"The laptop was encrypted, but I was able to retrieve the private key by performing a memory capture. The next step is to perform a full forensic analysis, which can take hours. Once this is done, special hardware and software are needed to determine what, if anything, is on that system," Mr. Henry said.

Agent Appleton didn't say anything for several moments.

"Can't I just view the files now that the laptop is unlocked?"

"Yes, but your evidence could potentially become spoiled by doing that!" Mr. Henry said in a cautious tone.

"Do you know anything about unlocking mobile devices?"

"Unfortunately, I do not, but I'm sure the FBI mobile lab can help you with that."

Agent Appleton thanked Mr. Henry for his help yet again, then departed.

Agent Appleton called the incident commander on duty at the forensics lab near Washington, D.C.

"Hello, this is Agent John Appleton working out of Milford."

"Watch Commander Davis. Do you have evidence to check in?"

"I do. Is there any possibility we can get a rush on processing evidence from a mobile device?"

"Do you have the code?"

"I do not, but I'm working under a clock."

"Is there any way you can get your suspect to unlock the phone?"

"I already tried that."

"Then, unfortunately, there is little I can do. You can send it in, but it will be a first-come, first-served basis."

"Wait, I also have evidence on a laptop. Is there any way you can get evidence off that?"

"Yes, but I'm afraid we are in the same situation as the mobile phone. We are understaffed, and our caseload is high."

Agent Appleton broke the connection and booted up the laptop. He quickly found a document related to burner phone bulk purchases. He also found a file with several links to Dark Web servers.

Several minutes later, Agent Appleton was able to secure a MORP connection to the Dark Web. He couldn't understand what the links were by looking at the names of the links. They seemed like random gibberish. One feature he did notice was that each extension ended with ".un."

Agent Appleton was just about to click on one of the links when he noticed a file called "ReadMe" on the desktop. He clicked on that file, and several links with descriptive text appeared. Then the screen went black.

As he checked the power connection to ensure that it was secure and connected to an outlet, he heard a distinctive beep which he recognized from when a system restarted.

"The computer probably just restarted after an update."

A white progress bar appeared on the screen. He waited patiently for the bar to disappear.

It didn't.

Approximately thirty minutes later, Agent Appleton returned to see: "No system or boot loader present."

Nigel knew that Jet had an online persona in *The Colossal Machine* named JetaGirl because JetGirl was already taken.

Nigel opened the game client for *The Colossal Machine*.

Since they had connected in-game previously, looking for her shouldn't have been difficult. Nigel appeared in his ante-room, a chamber where he could prepare for gameplay. Only players that had achieved certain social status were allowed anterooms.

Nigel checked his connection log; only four contacts appeared.

- Jet - Offline 10 Hours
- George - Offline 20 Days
- Milo - Offline 23 Hours
- Jake - Offline 13 Days

Nigel had hoped to catch Jet online. He decided to do the next best thing and send her an in-game message.

Dear Jet,

I wanted to properly thank you for saving my life. You risked yourself, your freedom, and your mobility to make sure that I survived the attack that has forever changed us. I regret any pain your brave actions caused you. My heart was broken when I saw you in the hospital. I didn't want to disturb your slumber, so I left you.

When I returned, you were gone.

I wish I had stayed.

Yours Truly and Friend Forever,

Nigel

Agent Appleton attempted to revive Rocky's computer several times to no avail. He had no idea why the computer wasn't rebooting. He reached for his phone and dialed.

"I thought you'd be contacting me again," Mr. Henry said.

"Are you around tonight?"

"I have a class at the store from six to eight. After that, I'm free."

"See you soon."

Agent Appleton waited until the remaining students filed out before entering. Mr. Henry was sitting behind the counter, reading the newspaper.

"Let me guess, you accessed that computer but still need help?" Mr. Henry said.

Agent Appleton placed the computer on the counter and gave a brief explanation of the problem. Mr. Henry looked concerned; he flipped the Wi-Fi switch on the side of the computer as a precaution.

"I'm afraid the hard drive inside the computer has been wiped."

"Can't you get the information back?"

"Depending on the storage medium, we might be able to get some fragments."

"What do you mean?"

"I suspect that a computer virus wiped out the computer. Based on your timeline, the hard drive was probably formatted in secure mode at least once. As the hard drive is formatted, each file is shredded; it often takes several passes before the data is unrecoverable."

Agent Appleton felt relieved. At least he had a chance to set things straight.

"I need to get this checked back into inventory tomorrow. Is that enough time?" Agent Appleton asked.

"Only if we work all night!"

"What can I do to help?"

"I think you helped enough, but you can wait here."

Mr. Henry left the room with the computer. *I'm racking up quite a few favors,* Agent Appleton thought.

Several hours later, Mr. Henry came out with a grim look on his face.

"The good news is that the hard drive was small, so I was able to create a 'bit' image. The bad news is that the drive is based on solid state technology."

"Why is that bad?" Agent Appleton asked.

Mr. Henry gave Agent Appleton a stern look.

"Unlike a traditional hard disk, solid state technology has built-in cleanup mechanisms. When something like a file is deleted, the drive will need to erase it before storing anything else."

"How much data can you retrieve from the drive? Can you

get it to boot?" Agent Appleton had some technical training, but he really didn't have a head for all of the jargon.

"I was able to restore much of the basic file structure, but the boot areas are unrecoverable."

Assignments from Collective Systems resumed. Nigel started to get a little worried; his access to Collective Systems resources was only possible during assignment windows. Nigel was learning that interns didn't enjoy the same privileges as full employees. Figures.

Nigel received some assignments from Collective Systems and two text messages at the same time, one from Milo and one from an unknown number. Nigel prioritized the texts before the assignments so the countdown didn't start.

Nigel opened the message from Milo first.

"Hey, Nige, how you doing? My sister Cassidy will be texting you soon. Her number is 555-3627. She won't tell me why she needs to talk, but I think she has a message from Jet. Not sure if you know this, but they have been friends for a couple of years now."

Sure enough, the unknown number matched Cassidy's.

"Hello, Nigel, you don't know me well, but we've met a couple of times when you were visiting Milo. We have a mutual friend, Josephine. She asked me to contact you since her father made her block all communication to your number. Jet is in the middle of packing. Her father is moving her out of the state. I will be meeting her tonight. She asked if I could contact you on her behalf."

Why does her father hate me? Nigel wondered.

While he pondered, Cassidy sent another message.

"So here is the plan. I'm going to Jet's house to say goodbye. We will have a short window for a video call on my phone. You will have five minutes to say goodbye. Please reply as soon as you get this text."

Nigel replied to Cassidy, saying that he would settle for a video call if that was the only way he could say goodbye. Several minutes later, Cassidy sent another text.

"We're all set. Can you talk now?"

Nigel glanced at his watch. He still had several minutes of grace time left before he had to accept or deny the assignment.

"Sure, I can talk now," Nigel replied.

Nigel's phone rang with the video call tone.

"Hello!?!"

Ahh, I sound weak and vulnerable! Nigel thought.

Seconds later, Jet appeared. Her pink streaks were gone. Her face looked off; Nigel couldn't place the expression. The camera on the phone panned, and he was able to see most of her body now. Cassidy must be controlling the phone.

"As you can see, I'm pretty messed up right now," Jet said. "I haven't been able to get on a computer to find you in-game, and my father is so angry. He blames you for the attack for some reason. I tried talking him out of it, but he wouldn't listen. I hope you don't mind that Cassidy is here with me."

"No! Not at all. I'm glad that someone is there," Nigel said.

That's not want I wanted to say. Nige, you are so stupid, Nigel thought.

Jet didn't seem to notice his awkward word choice. She winced and changed positions slightly, as if it was painful to even have this conversation.

Better make your next words count, Dummy!

"Jet, I sent you this in an in-game message, but I want to say it in person. You are the most selfless person I have ever known.

I just hope I can repay you someday. It is my deepest desire to see you again under different circumstances. I hope your father realizes how important you are. You are so very important to me."

Nigel wanted to say more, but the words seemed stuck in his throat. His eyes were getting blurry. Nigel wiped the tears from his eyes.

Jet abruptly took the phone from Cassidy with her good arm. Her expression changed; she looked as if someone hit her hard from behind. She pulled the phone close, and the image blurred. *Did she kiss the phone?* Nigel was perplexed as he mulled this over.

"I will get in touch when I can. Stay safe, my love," Jet said, then disconnected.

Nigel stared at his phone in stunned silence.

Nigel's phone alarm sounded. He realized that he only had two minutes before the grace period for accepting the assignments was ending. He opened the app, then accepted the assignment without looking.

Nigel's chest felt tight; he longed to have even one more minute with Jet.

As Nigel's mind began to clear, he read the assignment description—and wished he had read it before accepting it:

Greetings Nigel,

I hope this finds you well.

Collective Systems is pleased to offer you the following assignment.

Title: Recon Mission

Need reconnaissance performed on a local target. The

proprietor of Better Buy Computers is a person of interest for The Collective. Please provide information on his daily routine. This individual has served in both the U.S. Federal Bureau of Investigation (FBI) and the National Security Agency (NSA). Proceed with caution.

Nigel was stunned. *Mr. Henry?*

Nigel received two more alerts on his phone, both from the Collective Systems app.

"RECALL FAILED: Recon Mission."

"Assignment sent in error, automation failed, please manually delete messages from app."

Nigel performed the requested actions, then tapped the verify button.

"APP VERIFICATION IN PROGRESS. DO NOT TURN OFF."

Several minutes later, he was able to access the app normally. The assignment was gone.

What just happened?

Nigel was confounded; not only did he receive conflicting information about an assignment, but the nature of the assignment seemed very illegal. Nigel was determined to get to the bottom of this. He picked up the phone and dialed Natasha.

"I'm so sorry," Natasha said when she picked up. "You received the wrong assignment. Sometimes the automated system gets garbled and sends the wrong information."

Nigel frowned.

"That is only partially why I called. The assignment described my friend, Mr. Henry, in detail, and it wanted me to eavesdrop on his business. I didn't sign up to be a snitch."

"Clearly, you're upset. I will get to the bottom of this mix-up and call you back soon."

Natasha attempted to contact Alexei, but his assistant informed her that he was unavailable. She contacted Viktor instead.

"There is a problem with assignments that are being sent to interns. Something is wrong. Dispatch is redacting, canceling, or amending assignments."

The Collective's systems had worked for years without so much as a hiccup. Viktor suspected that Gregor was behind this somehow.

Based on the security access data, the interns produced a model where Gregor was in the 99th percentile as being a person of interest in the database hack.

Viktor picked up the phone and called the Cray Group, an independent research firm that specialized in big data analysis.

"Hello, I'm making an inquiry of a big data report that I requested over a week ago."

"Please hold, Sir."

Viktor checked the time in California where the group was based. It was well within business hours, so he felt confident.

"Viktor?"

"I'm here."

"Hello, I'm Dr. Anderson. I'm in charge of the group that is doing the analysis."

"Why is it taking so long to get the results?"

"We are actually finishing your report now, but it will be several more days until it's completed."

"Is the analysis part done?"

"Yes. It just takes time for a writer to finish the report. I wouldn't consider it complete until that happens."

"Doctor, I need the data. You need to send me an unofficial report, no matter how crude it looks. Immediately."

"That's not our policy!"

"I don't care about your policy. My boss is looking to eliminate an ongoing threat."

"I see. Hold, please."

After several more minutes, the doctor finally agreed to send an unofficial report to Viktor by the end of his day. That would be very late for Viktor, but he had little choice. He would wait.

Agent Appleton's phone rang a little after 2 a.m.

"This better be good."

"I figured out the rest of the encryption from the data you provided, and it is all accessible," Mr. Henry said.

"I thought you said that the encryption was unbreakable."

"Takes time, but it is not impossible. Turns out the author wrote his own encryption routines, which is frankly the only reason I was able to crack it at all."

"Did you find anything useful?"

"I haven't looked at it. I wanted to give you the honors."

Agent Appleton made it to Mr. Henry's house shortly after sunrise. Mr. Henry opened the door as soon as Agent Appleton got out of his car.

"I went through the data while you were en route and found Rocky has several connections to the IP addresses you supplied. I was able to access a backup of his phone and was able to harvest several contacts."

Mr. Henry led Agent Appleton into his kitchen, where he gestured to a partial diagram on a whiteboard. In the center, a town graphic appeared with lines pointing to names such as Natasha, Nigel, and Tage.

"Who are these people?"

"They have the most contact with our buddy, Rocky."

Agent Appleton made a sketch of Mr. Henry's whiteboard.

"Milford seems to be the epicenter of all activity. Nigel is linked to several of the IP addresses that I gave you, while Rocky has physical links," Agent Appleton said. "But what does it mean?"

The deputy director's deadline was fast approaching and Agent Appleton had little to show for it. Agent Appleton's new plan was simple: offer Rocky a deal in exchange for key information and testimony. Nigel didn't seem to be important, but Agent Appleton would put that theory to the test if he didn't get results.

Back at home, Agent Appleton entered in all relevant data that Mr. Henry gathered from his decryption efforts. The FBI crimes database provided relevant police reports or other interesting information based on name, location, and other identifying markers. The more information that Agent Appleton provided, the more possible matches he would get from the database.

He discovered Nigel Watson was reportedly involved in a shooting incident in Milford recently. Two red flags came to mind. Nigel has the same last name as Ellen, a friend of Sally Lewis, with whom he attended high school. If Nigel was involved with The Collective, that could explain Ellen's hacking. Agent Appleton made a note to follow up with this connection, but for now the shooting incident was the most interesting. He pulled up Detective Foster's report, which contained the facts as well as some personal observations that Nigel was being evasive. Two other teenagers were also involved but didn't seem suspicious.

Other recoverable information found on the laptop led

Agent Appleton to an app on Rocky's phone. Although encryption was used, an additional IP address found in the logs revealed another point of entry for The Collective's infrastructure. Agent Appleton was able to make additional correlations using an FBI database and found several that led to Nigel Watson. This was the evidence that he needed to implicate and create a connection to Rocky.

Time to pay Nigel a visit.

Late that evening, Viktor received the unofficial report from the Cray Group. Alexei asked Viktor to call once he had time to analyze the results. Viktor didn't understand any of the machine learning or quantifiable analysis used in the report, but he did understand language that made someone guilty. The Cray Group wholeheartedly agreed with the interns.

"What did you find out?" Alexei asked over the phone.

"The group you recommended agreed with our interns. Gregor is guilty. Gregor's IP was captured several times before and after intrusion attempts. Our party boy is getting sloppy," Viktor said.

"Burn him, but don't eliminate him. I want to teach him a lesson. Also, give our interns a congratulatory bonus."

"It will be done."

Agent Appleton traced the app IP address to an address on 302 Sycamore Lane in Milford—Ellen's house, as suspected. There were several Wi-Fi signals emanating from the home; however, one was unusually strong. No other house in the area had Wi-Fi signals nearly as strong.

He stepped onto the porch and rang the bell. This was going to be an interesting conversation.

Ellen Watson answered the door.

"Hello, Agent. Come inside. Do you have news on the hackers?" Ellen asked in a hopeful voice.

"No, I'm here to see your son, Nigel," Agent Appleton said.

"Nigel? What could you possibly want with him?"

"All I can tell you is that he is a person of interest in an ongoing investigation."

"Nige, come down here, please," Ellen yelled.

A few minutes later, Nigel appeared.

"Agent Appleton has a few questions to ask you," Ellen said.

"Do you work for Collective Systems?" Agent Appleton asked.

Ellen interrupted. "Yes, he got a paid internship there. It was a godsend since I was left with little money when I got hacked."

Agent Appleton nodded. "What do you do for Collective Systems?"

Nigel described his position as a Level Five intern. He recounted the weekend at Tage Manor as well as some of the assignments, but omitted the mix-up with Mr. Henry's assignment.

"How do you get these assignments?"

Nigel demonstrated the app.

Agent Appleton said nothing for almost a minute. He could see that Nigel was visibly nervous.

"Nigel Watson, you are under arrest for crimes related to the Computer Fraud and Abuse Act."

"What the hell?!" Ellen said.

Ellen stood between Nigel and Agent Appleton.

"We have evidence that Nigel has knowingly committed

crimes while working for an organization known as The Collective."

"You mean Collective Systems?" Nigel asked. "I told you, I have an internship there."

"You really think you're working for a legitimate company?" Agent Appleton asked. He decided to hear Nigel out.

Nigel told him everything that he had been involved with through the past several weeks, including the hacking, exploitation, and reconnaissance efforts to get Jake's account unlocked.

"I have your IP address associated with systems belonging to a criminal organization known as The Collective. Their front is a gaming company called Pretzelverse Games."

"That doesn't make sense. I have only played games produced by Pretzelverse Games, not developed for them. The company I intern for is Collective Systems; it's not a criminal organization."

"What specific work have you done?"

"Most of it was debugging existing programs that didn't work, or writing code to integrate machine learning algorithms."

Nigel also showed Agent Appleton his computer and VPN software that he used to connect to Collective Systems, Inc. The VPN software had the company's logo on it.

"How do you communicate with your contacts at Collective Systems?"

Nigel showed Agent Appleton the app's messaging feature and shared Natasha's contact information.

"I need to see your completed assignments."

"The links to complete the assignments expire after a period of time, so I can't show you. My VPN software only works when I have an active assignment."

Agent Appleton considered for a very long time, then made a phone call on the porch. Several minutes later, he reentered the house with officers from the Milford Police Department. Nigel was handcuffed and read his Miranda rights.

"Wait! You're not taking my boy." Ellen stood in front of the arresting officers.

"Please move, Ma'am." Agent Appleton pulled Ellen away. The officers removed Nigel.

CHAPTER 22

GREGOR RECEIVED a code from dispatch that instructed him to call the head of The Collective. Gregor established the secure link, then dialed Alexei's private line.

"Greetings, Gregor," Alexei said.

"Why have you summoned me? I'm running point on a very sensitive mission."

"Is that the second attempt at Nigel's life?" Alexei said in a matter-of-fact tone. Gregor said nothing. "I also need you to put a stop to this. I will not tolerate betrayal."

"I have not betrayed you. My actions have only increased the security of The Collective," Gregor said.

"No, your actions have only succeeded in doing *harm* to The Collective," Alexei said.

"The real threat was Rocky, who allowed his laptop to be found and used by the FBI to confirm The Collective's existence. He probably spilled his guts to the American authorities."

"Yes, it was unfortunate that Rocky got picked up, but he didn't betray The Collective," Alexei said. "An operative will meet you at your designated safe house in Minsk to relieve you of your access codes and company-owned equipment."

"Before you send the operative, please consider my point of view. Can we discuss in person?" Gregor said.

Alexei didn't immediately respond.

"Gregor, you have been like a son to me. I will give you one chance to explain yourself. Instructions will follow," Alexei said as he hung up.

Hopefully, that bought some time, Gregor thought.

As the sun rose in Chechnya, Gregor perched at his computer like a vulture waiting for something to die. During the evening, he transferred one hundred million in Digibit to several unmarked wallets located in several regions across the world.

Gregor planned to be in the wind within the hour. "It's done," Gregor said to himself. He added his laptop to his go bag. As soon as it was zipped, he noticed Natasha.

"Hello, Love!" Natasha said.

"Are you here to burn me?"

"That depends!"

"On what?"

"Show me the proof that your second attempt to kill Nigel is called off."

"Why is this kid so important?"

"Alexei hoped you and Nigel would work together, as brothers."

Gregor produced the chat logs that confirmed that the hit was redacted. Natasha looked them over.

"You involved Black Iris?"

"Yes, they run the Dark Web forums that make it possible for these things to happen. They have a great reputation."

Natasha didn't like this; it didn't feel right.

"Sorry, my darling, but examples must be made."

She pulled the trigger. A small dart pierced the skin on Gregor's neck. He tried reaching for the dart, but everything went dark very fast.

Nigel was thrown into a small holding room, followed by Agent Appleton.

"Have a seat, Nigel."

Nigel sat in one of the chairs that were next to a table. He looked into the mirror that hung on the opposite wall. He saw a vulnerable and scared kid. Not the confident young man he felt like while with his friends.

Agent Appleton opened a folder and put several pictures on the table.

"I need you to identify these criminals for me."

Agent Appleton pointed to a picture of a very large man with a bald head who didn't seem to have a neck. He looked like a bouncer.

"I don't know him."

Agent Appleton pointed at a picture of a woman with mean and unforgiving eyes and striking black hair.

"She looks familiar, but I don't know her."

"Well, that's strange," Agent Appleton said. "You were seen with both of these people at the same time."

"What? That isn't possible. I don't know these people."

Agent Appleton produced another higher quality photo with Nigel getting in a car with Natasha. Rocky was holding the door open.

"They don't look like the people in the previous photos," Nigel said.

Agent Appleton gathered the phones and left the room.

Cassidy was in her room preparing for midterm exams when she received the next wave of text messages.

"The Mensch is Down, please respond."

Cassidy opened her drawer where she kept her important papers. The envelope labeled "Mensch" was opened. Her heart skipped a beat when she pulled out the folder that contained Nigel's picture. She flipped the picture and texted back the code on the back of the picture. As she waited for a response, she could hardly believe that Nigel was the Mensch. That title was reserved for the intern of the decade.

Her phone chimed again.

"Awaken the sleepers."

Cassidy looked for another sealed envelope; she pulled out the one labeled "Sleepers." That folder contained the contact sheets of several more pictures, including her brother Milo and Mr. Robinson. She texted the codes to awaken the operatives for the next phase of the operation.

Cassidy didn't know this, but awakening the sleepers set in motion a series of events, all designed to help a fellow intern.

Mr. Robinson walked into the precinct of the Milford Police Department.

"Hello, Commander," Mr. Robinson said as he passed his desk.

"Hi, James. I didn't know you were working tonight!"

"Yup, coming in late due to a mess at the high school."

After a few minutes of preparation, Mr. Robinson did some reconnaissance down the hall where the holding rooms were. The information he received was that Nigel was held in the last room on the left, close to where the hall ended. Mr. Robinson waited until the coast was clear, then quickly opened Nigel's holding room door. Nigel's head was buried in his hands. As

Nigel's head came up, Mr. Robinson slapped a small piece of paper into his hand.

"Hey, you're not supposed to be in there," a uniformed officer said, poking her head into the room.

"Sorry, I was just cleaning. Thought these were empty."

After Mr. Robinson left, the officer shut the door and locked it.

A small paper folded several times over was in the palm of Nigel's hand. He carefully opened it.

"Hang in there, Kid. Help is coming. Say nothing. The FBI has nothing on you. Eat this paper immediately after reading."

Nigel did as instructed, but was baffled as to why Mr. Robinson gave it to him.

Hunter Garrison checked the forums for available bounties in the eastern United States. Since he was a founding member of Black Iris, he had certain site privileges, like reactivating canceled contracts. Of all the recently canceled contracts, Nigel's looked the easiest and most promising. His location was only a few hours away; he was young and lived in a smaller community.

Hunter's brief research into court records found that Nigel was currently arrested on suspicion of hacking.

Hunter configured his computer to scan the IP range of all addresses in the Milford area. His port scan revealed vulnerable cameras operated near the precinct building. He found visible precinct coverage on a hardware store, grocery store, and pharmacy, and configured each camera to upload recordings.

Agent Appleton received a call with a small lock icon next to an unknown number. The connection was encrypted, which could only mean official agency business.

"Agent Appleton speaking."

"Comrade, I have a proposition for you," the mysterious voice said. Agent Appleton thought that the voice had a subtle Russian accent but wasn't sure.

"Who is this?"

"Consider me a mutual friend. You have someone in custody that I want released."

"Who might that be?"

"Nigel Watson."

Agent Appleton was intrigued.

"What do I get in return?"

"You get a hacker who is responsible for stealing thousands of American identities, creating accounts, then selling the merchandise for profit. I think you are getting the better end of the bargain."

"What is your interest in this kid?"

"Let's just say that I see his full potential."

Agent Appleton considered, then nodded. "You got a deal."

Alexei hung up the phone.

He delivered Gregor gift-wrapped on the steps of the local FBI field office. He was tied up with green and red rope. His mouth was stuffed with a small Christmas stocking, held in place with holiday tape. A note was taped to Gregor that read:

"A gift for Agent Appleton. Do open before Christmas. Happy Holidays!"

A USB flash drive was taped to the note. When Agent Appleton examined the flash drive, he realized that it was encrypted. He didn't want to bother Mr. Henry again, especially during Thanksgiving weekend, but he had to know what was on the drive.

He drove to Milford and asked for Mr. Henry.

"What do you want?" Mr. Henry said in a cold voice.

"Can you please help me with another encryption problem?" Agent Appleton asked in a good-natured tone. He considered Mr. Henry a friend. He thought they developed some rapport over these past weeks.

"Nigel Watson is a good kid. You should consider releasing him," Mr. Henry said.

Agent Appleton raised his eyebrows.

"Good day, Agent Appleton!" Mr. Henry said as he closed the door on him.

"I will see what I can do to get him released," Agent Appleton said to the closed door. Mr. Henry didn't respond.

Several days after his arrest, Nigel was still incarcerated. Ellen hired an attorney without using a recommendation from Sally or anyone else. She found Julius Shcherbakov, Esquire, in Newport, the next town over. Julius promised to work with Agent Appleton and believed that he could have Nigel released within the next twenty-four hours.

"The FBI's case is weak. All of the evidence is circumstantial," Julius said.

Ellen felt assured that Julius was working on Nigel's behalf. She had sold her only vehicle, her jewelry, and other valuable items to help pay for Nigel's defense. She also thought about getting another job.

"You should set up a fundraiser page to help raise the additional funds," Julius suggested. "I will help you."

With Julius's help, Ellen was able to craft a message for the crowdfunding website:

"Nigel Watson is an honor student and takes time away from his studies to help others. His grades have guaranteed an internship for a large software company. My son has been wrongly arrested for crimes of computer hacking he did not commit. The FBI has failed to provide sufficient evidence, so I demand my son be released immediately. Please help my son and donate whatever you can to aid in his defense."

A copy of the *Milford Gazette* was left at Ellen's front door. *That is odd. I don't subscribe to the paper.* She opened it, and a note fell to the ground which read, "Go to the circled section, bottom of the fold."

The circled section read: "FBI Targets Honor Student.

"In a desperate attempt to gain a conviction, the FBI mistakenly incarcerated a young honor student whose name is withheld because the student is a minor. The student in question has yet to be charged and has been incarcerated for more than a week. 'We intend to seek damages for the student's wrongful arrest and conviction unless the student is immediately released,' Julius Shcherbakov, the student's attorney, said."

Agent Appleton was called into the deputy director's office.

"Explain your actions concerning the unauthorized detainment of a minor," the deputy director demanded.

"I have proof that ties Mr. Watson's IP address to the hacker I picked up."

The deputy director didn't seem to care. "I've been told that the family has lost nearly everything and they may have grounds to sue. This is unacceptable and unbecoming of an agent. You are suspended with pay until we can sort all of this out. Surrender your badge and firearm before leaving this office!"

Agent Appleton was in shock. He was escorted to central processing, where he had to turn in his badge, firearm, and FBI-issued phone.

Just after former Agent John Appleton was signing the receipt for the official items, his personal phone rang. The caller was from an unknown number.

"Hello," John said.

"This is only the beginning, Agent Appleton. Or should I call you John now?" The call ended with an audible click.

CHAPTER 23

HUNTER REVIEWED the video footage from the past few days. He noticed that officers and other civilian workers were departing from an unseen location. While he didn't have eyes on the actual door, he noticed that some workers would enter the front of the precinct, then exit from the rear of the building in an alleyway of some kind.

Perfect cover.

Hunter drove by the Milford Police Station to get a feel for the place. Several officers were gathered in front of the precinct, many of them talking, smoking, or drinking coffee. He parked in an alley behind the hardware store. The precinct was just one block up and another alleyway over. He gathered his pole-climbing tools, then headed toward the adjacent side alley.

Hunter looked like any other telecommunications line worker. No one even gave him a second glance as he climbed the telephone pole and mounted a wireless camera. He concealed himself behind a junction box. Once he was satisfied that the camera wouldn't be easily noticed, he gathered his equipment, checked the camera's feed, and left the area. Hunter now had eyes on the back exit.

Hunter received an alert from the webpage tracker code he

installed. The Milford court docket had changed; it appeared that Nigel now had a court date. A quick check of the online court docket revealed the courthouse and judge. The room wasn't sealed, which meant that anyone could visit the hearing. Hunter was planning on attending.

"I'm here to see my client," Julius said to the front desk of the Milford Police Department. "Nigel Watson."

The duty chief buzzed in Julius. "He has been moved to the conference room near the back of the precinct. Give this to the guard on duty."

The duty chief handed the authorization slip to Julius. Since Nigel was a minor, the Milford police had a legal obligation to separate him from any adult that was incarcerated. Apparently all of the holding cells and interview rooms were full if Nigel was in a conference room.

"How you holding up, Kid?"

Nigel's head was buried in the sleeves of his hoodie. Several snacks, sandwich wrappers, and a toiletry pack were visible on the table.

"The good news is that you have an actual court date tomorrow. We have an excellent chance of getting you released."

Nigel's head snapped up with a small smile, the first sign of joy he had seen on the kid's face.

"Legally, the court had to see you within twenty-one days of arrest. You're at ten days, but I convinced a judge to move it up sooner since you were denied visitors for the first several days."

Julius handed Nigel a paper and pen.

"Write down your suit size. We're going to court!"

Hunter's strategy was to take care of Nigel before he appeared in court. Based on the court documents he was able to exfiltrate, the prisoner would be transported to the courthouse via a waiting vehicle in the back alley. The perfect spot for an ambush.

Hunter walked the length of the alleyway. There were no potential hiding spots even remotely close to the back door of the police station. However, there was a dumpster behind the hardware store five hundred feet away from the door. That would have to do.

The dumpster provided good cover. Hunter waited there in an oversized appliance box in a coat that he purchased from an actual homeless person for $20 and a bottle of cheap wine. After rubbing some dirt on his face, he looked like any other homeless man in America.

Hunter heard a car turning the corner toward the police precinct. Time to move.

He rounded the corner just as the precinct door opened. Nigel Watson appeared in a full suit, accompanied by his attorney and a uniformed police officer. Another officer waited in the car.

Hunter quickly pulled out an object the size of a tennis ball and hurled it toward the vehicle. There was a loud banging noise, followed by a puff of smoke. Hunter pulled small knives from his coat and threw several in quick succession. The officer escorting Nigel took a knife in the throat, and blood gushed out. The officer stumbled, withdrew the knife, dropped to his knees, then slumped over.

Nigel dropped to the ground—he felt a sharp pain in his right bicep. A small knife was embedded in the muscle. Another knife penetrated his left side with an explosion of pain. Nigel screamed as the pain washed over him. It felt worse than anything he had ever experienced, even more than the bullet graze. Beside the police car, a man appeared with knives in each hand, several smaller knives in his belt. Lying at his feet was the officer from the car and his attorney. He had no idea if either one was alive.

There was blood everywhere.

Detective Foster was in his office writing a report when he heard a loud sound. He recognized the sound as a flashbang and immediately started making his way toward it. The hallway leading to the back door was deserted. Prisoners were in the holding cells shouting, even louder than normal. At the end of the hallway, Detective Foster heard muffled cries from the other side of the door. He pulled out his service weapon and crouched, then flung the door open.

He took in the bloody scene before him. At least four people were down, and a lone man in a ragged coat hovered over a kid in a suit. The man's back obscured part of the view, but Detective Foster noticed the gleam of a large knife pressed against the kid's throat. Detective Foster's eyes widened when he recognized Nigel.

"Stop!"

The figure proceeded to cut. Detective Foster shot the figure several times in the back. The figure slumped over, then began to move. *A vest!* The figure turned, and Foster was met with the piercing intensity of the figure's eyes. His face was concealed with a mask that appeared to be a burlap sack with eye holes cut out. A second later, Detective Foster was hit in the chest with a small throwing knife.

"Your weapons cannot harm me. Cower before me,

Mortal," the figure growled. Foster turned onto his back. Blood gushed from his wound and mouth. He couldn't breathe. He struggled to stay awake. Three uniformed officers appeared and gave chase; another stayed with the carnage and called for backup.

The figure had too much of a lead on the pursuing officers. He rounded the corner of the only possible exit. The coat and mask were left behind. The officers split up, determined to find the perpetrator that attacked their own. Officer Anderson's endurance began to flag. He stopped to have a look around.

"Any sign?" the other pursuing officer said.

"None!"

Police blocked off streets within two blocks around the precinct. Ambulances were the only vehicles allowed through. Officers checked the street, each car and every building, inside and out. When pedestrians were interviewed, no suspects were discovered, which only heightened the tension of the Milford police.

Officer Anderson decided to walk Main Street one last time before giving up. It was subtle at first—a tree about fifty feet away shook unnaturally. It was just outside the perimeter. Officer Anderson squelched his radio, then approached from the street, which provided some cover from parked cars. Officer Anderson inspected the suspect tree and saw a man dressed all in black clinging to the trunk of the tree.

"Come down from there!"

Officer Anderson dodged a throwing knife and fired at one of the perpetrator's legs. The perpetrator moved, but not before getting grazed by the bullet. Hunter groaned in agony but didn't leave the tree. Officer Anderson attempted to call for backup. A lasso of nylon rope was thrown over his neck and tightened as the perpetrator pulled upward. Officer Anderson attempted to aim the weapon again, but he couldn't breathe. Officer Anderson grabbed the rope with both hands, dropping the pistol. The perpetrator looked like a kid, eighteen or nineteen at most. That was the last thing Officer Anderson remembered before he passed out.

Hunter vacated the area before reinforcements arrived.

Nigel awoke to the sound of machines. He opened his eyes and discovered that he was yet again in the hospital. His mother, brother, and attorney were in the room. Julius's head and arm were wrapped. Nigel tried to speak, and only a gurgling sound came out. He touched his throat. It was taped, and a tube was protruding.

"Don't speak, Honey. The doctors performed a tracheotomy."

Ellen turned away. Nigel could hear her sobbing.

Once she regained some composure, Ellen gave Nigel a pad of paper and a pen. He wrote, "What happened?"

"The Milford Police Precinct was attacked," Julius said. "They're still looking for the suspect. He threw knives at us, like he had martial arts training. Two officers died from their injuries. Detective Foster is in surgery but is expected to make it. Another officer was hung, it appears. The suspect didn't have time to finish the job. I believe he will make it. I was grazed by a couple knives; another plunged into my arm. Other than that, I'm okay," Julius said.

John Appleton walked into the room.

"Agent Appleton, what brings you down here?" Ellen asked.

"I don't think you should be here," Julius said at the same time.

"I drove down as soon as I heard. I want to lend a hand if I can. I'm here as a friend, not as an agent of the FBI," John said.

"You're not an agent," Julius said.

"Suspended pending review," John corrected. "Mistakes were made, but I will do what I can to rectify the situation."

Nigel raised his hand, then wrote, "Let him help."

"The FBI has two suspects in custody. Both have direct ties to Nigel.

One of them is a hacker."

"Who is this mystery hacker? Why don't I know about him?" Julius demanded.

"His name is Gregor, and he was a member of the hacker group called The Collective. Not to be confused with Collective Systems, which has been verified as a legitimate business," John said.

Nigel frowned. He recognized the name, but didn't want John Appleton to know.

"I'm owed some favors at the Bureau. I will see how the case against Gregor is progressing," John said.

Julius handed Agent Appleton his card.

"Please keep in touch."

John Appleton wasn't sure if Janice would help, but she did owe him a favor.

"If I can do it, I will," she said over the phone. "But things have changed around here since you left."

"How so?"

"The deputy director is making agents more accountable for evidence collection. A no-tolerance policy for bypassing the system."

"Why are you telling me this?"

"Because your work is the example of what not to do."

"Harsh," John said. "Has Gregor Gobechov given us anything?"

"The deputy director let him go a few days after you were suspended. Let me find out why. Hold, please."

John Appleton's brow furrowed. This wouldn't have happened on his watch. A few minutes later, Janice returned.

"'Improper evidence collection' and 'unauthorized examination of evidence' are the reasons given," Janice said.

"What about Rocky?"

"Who?"

"Rocco Surelli."

John heard a series of keystrokes.

"He was released as well, citing the exact same reasons," Janice said.

"What about Nigel Watson?"

"He is still under investigation but is expected to be released. His lawyer is insisting that the case be dropped. I know the deputy director wants all of this to go away."

John thanked Janice, then hung up. He was back where he started!

John returned to the hospital. Nigel was asleep. Ellen was trying to rest in a nearby chair. He wished he could take it all back. This family had been through a lot in such a short time.

Ellen opened her eyes. "Did the hacker talk?" she asked hopefully.

John didn't want to bring her more bad news, especially now that her son was injured, but didn't see the point in lying about it, either.

"No, he was released."

All of her bottled-up emotions overwhelmed her, and she started weeping uncontrollably. John put his hand on her shoulder to try and comfort her.

Nigel clapped his hands, then waved a piece of paper. John took it from Nigel and read:

"I think I know who Gregor is. There may be a connection between The Collective. Get Julius. We should talk."

"Great news," Julius said as he entered the room. "The FBI has agreed to drop all charges and pay some restitution. The details will be forthcoming."

Nigel smiled. Ellen gave Nigel a hug as tears rolled down her face.

Nigel relayed the accidental communication that he received on the Collective Systems app. Nigel provided John with additional information on how his machine learning research had led to Gregor being found out as a traitor to Collective Systems. Nigel didn't think that Gregor's capture by the FBI was a coincidence.

"Your suspicions are correct, Nigel. Gregor was hand-delivered to the FBI. He was wrapped like a Christmas present," John said.

"How convenient. It looks like you were played," Julius said. "I'm going to see that the FBI makes good on their promises. I want legal documents drawn this afternoon."

"Dispatch. What is your code word or phrase?"

"Black Heart," Julius said.

Julius was transferred directly to Alexei.

"Boss, it looks like Gregor has started a war with Black Iris."

"According to my research, Gregor created a bounty on the Black Iris board but later recanted. After Gregor's apprehension, it was discovered that Gregor hacked their site and stole vast amounts of Digibit held in escrow for other bounties. Gregor also set Nigel up again. The kid was nearly killed this time. They sent Hunter!"

Alexei said nothing for a long time.

"We need to meet with the opposition leaders and explain that Gregor is a rogue agent."

"Already on it, Boss!"

Using covert channels, Julius was able to set up a meeting between a high-ranking member of Black Iris and The Collective. Only two members of each side were allowed. Alexei chose Julius to represent him as his second. The meeting was to take place physically on neutral ground.

"It is done. The meeting will be held on Phantom Island in two days," Julius said.

"That will take at least a full day of travel, so we better leave soon."

Julius immediately headed to the airport and booked the first flight to Lisbon. He met Alexei at the airport. Julius sent the secure beacon from his burner phone. Within minutes, his phone rang.

"Your car is waiting, Mr. Shcherbakov. Ensure that Breven is with you."

"Ten-four, good buddy," Julius said.

An unremarkable black sedan pulled up. The driver stared at Julius for a moment, then signaled for them to enter. The back of the car had tinted windows. As soon as Alexei and Julius jumped in the car, the windows polarized. They couldn't see anything outside after that. Approximately thirty minutes later, the car pulled onto a boat and the voyage began.

"Merry Christmas, Boss."

Alexei was not in a celebratory mood, but he acknowledged Julius's good-natured attempt at cheering him up.

About an hour into the journey, the doors unlocked. Julius opened his side of the vehicle. He could see the ocean waves smashing the side of the vessel they were on. Smoke billowed about the deck as the wind changed positions. Soon, a large man approached them.

"Hello, I'm Captain Ramsey, captain of the Shadowstar." He held out a large black hand. Julius shook it and made introductions on The Collective side.

"What happened to you?"

"Part of what must be discussed with our mutual friends."

"I see."

"Come up to my captain's quarters. I have tea and scones waiting."

"Lead the way."

Captain Ramsey led them to his quarters. Alexei's stomach growled as he smelled the scones. The captain poured three cups of tea.

"Phantom Island is about a day's sail west," Captain Ramsey said. "The actual location of the island is a bit tricky to find. It is deserted, but has some passable roads. It is our Bermuda Triangle. Instruments go haywire, and you can only navigate by the stars. We will get to the edge of the chop, drop anchor, then wait for nightfall. The Shadow Dealers have many remote outposts. We have settled disputes between criminal organizations for years."

Ramsey chuckled.

Alexei had a strange feeling as enjoyed his tea and scones.

"Where is Black Iris?" Alexei asked.

"They were picked up by another vessel and will meet us on the island. We do this for everyone's protection," Captain Ramsey explained.

Alexei nodded.

"Now that we have broken bread together, we should go over the rules."

"Will Black Iris be forced to follow the same rules?" Julius asked.

"Everyone does. Offending members will be blacklisted and their reputation tarnished!

"The rules are as follows: One, no communication with anyone not on the island under any circumstances. Two, participants must not interrupt each other during opening statements. Three, if a resolution cannot be made within seventy-two hours, both parties must agree to a five-week truce before negotiations will begin anew. During this time, no communication or business between parties shall commence. Four, the Shadow Dealers get paid no matter the outcome. Five, declarations of war must be made off Shadow Dealers' territory.

"Do you agree to these terms?"

"Yes," Julius said.

"Agreed," Alexei said.

"Now for the legal stuff."

Captain Ramsey produced a long scroll that looked ancient. Alexei and Julius signed the document. Captain Ramsey reviewed it, then placed it back in its protective covering.

"You will receive a copy once we arrive at the island. No copy machine here."

Dusk would be upon the vessel soon. The waves were getting rough. The ship was not small by any means, but it was beginning to get tossed around like a toy.

"Time to change navigation," Captain Ramsey said.

Alexei and Julius followed Captain Ramsey onto the deck of the Shadowstar. They could barely keep their balance due to the torrent of waves and rain.

"Where did this weather come from?" Alexei shouted.

"Our Triangle! Now get inside!" Captain Ramsey bellowed.

By the time the members of The Collective were back in the cabin, they were drenched. Alexei remembered Captain Ramsey saying that he navigated by the stars and wondered how that was possible in their current predicament. Several minutes later, the weather stopped as abruptly as it started. Alexei stepped outside and couldn't believe his eyes. The night sky was completely clear, and there were more stars than he had ever seen in one sky. Alexei was mesmerized.

Alexei opened his eyes as sunlight shone through the cabin. He could hear the rumbling sound of the engine and seagulls. He felt rested and at peace for the first time in a long time. He stepped out onto the deck and realized that they were docked. He could see a black sedan in the distance. Julius was leaning on one side of the car.

"Did you sleep well?" Captain Ramsey asked.

"Incredibly well."

"Good, you will need the rest for the trials to come."

Captain Ramsey extended a hand. They shook for several seconds.

"Good luck, my friend. I hope we meet again, under better circumstances."

"Thanks for your hospitality and safe passage, Captain."

Alexei walked to the sedan where Julius waited. He felt optimism for the first time in years.

"Ready to go, Boss?"

"Yes. I'm eager to get started."

As soon as Alexei and Julius were seated, the car started moving. The scenery was barren and bleak. Large rocks protruded in several places along the rough road. The vehicle shook as the cement turned into gravel.

"Not the paradise you were expecting?" Julius asked.

"This island looks deserted."

"I assure you it is not," the driver said. "There are all manner of creatures here, ranging from wild jackals to a variety of reptiles. Wandering off, especially at night, can be fatal."

"Good to know. I didn't get your name?"

"Roscoe," the driver replied.

The sedan started its ascent up a steep hill, and the width of the road decreased dramatically. The sedan stopped several hundred feet above sea level. Roscoe opened the passenger door. Alexei stepped out onto a surface that resembled blacktop.

Roscoe led them to a plain wall with no visible entry point. He pushed a brick, which revealed a handle, which in turn revealed a downward spiral staircase. Alexei and Julius followed Roscoe down the narrow staircase thirty feet. Roscoe led them to a large room that resembled a waiting area. Two couches and a coffee table were visible.

"You must be hungry after your voyage. We have prepared a meal for you," Roscoe said.

The next room contained a large rectangular table and twelve chairs. Several lamps illuminated the room. Two place settings were made at the far side of the table. Alexei and Julius took their places at the table. Between the place settings was an empty chair.

"Good morning, Gentlemen. My name is Malcolm. I'm your host for the gathering. Breakfast will be served momentarily. After that, I will show you to your quarters."

As soon as Malcolm finished speaking, a plate of bacon and over-easy eggs was placed in front of Alexei. A plate with a bagel, cream cheese, and lox was placed in front of Julius. Alexei and Julius shared a puzzled look.

"How did you know what we like?"

"The Shadow Dealers always do our homework," Malcolm said. "Now eat, and when you're finished I will give you the grand tour!"

Alexei devoured the breakfast in record time and was finished before Julius had finished the first half of his bagel. As promised, Malcolm gave Alexei and Julius a tour of the facility, which was inside the wall of a cliff. Alexei thought he could see his reflection in the polished stone of the walls and floors. The tour ended at the guest quarters.

"Is there Wi-Fi available?" Julius asked.

Malcolm glared at Julius as if he had cursed.

"No, I'm afraid this facility is in a no-Wi-Fi zone. A cocktail reception with all meeting participants will be held in the main hall at five sharp. Please, do not be late."

Alexei unpacked his two suits he brought for the negotiations, as he had found that dressing the part of a leader was essential. He wanted to look perfect. Despite being carved into a cliff, the room was bright. He went over to close the drapes and stopped. He was greeted by a spectacular view of the Atlantic Ocean. Far below, he could see vegetation and a small lake. He closed the drapes, then drifted off to sleep.

Julius woke Alexei at 3 p.m.

"I think we should go over our talking points," Julius said.

"Okay, advise me."

Julius inspected his notes for a moment.

"Okay, the first point is that you should admit no wrongdoing. You didn't know about any malicious activity Gregor was involved with. An important consideration is that Gregor was acting solo, with no known accomplices. If the conversation is going well and you want to be generous, offer a list of Gregor's known and unknown haunts. Oh, one other point—we should ask them for evidence of the hack and what brought it to their attention."

Alexei memorized all talking points.

"I hope you brought a suit for the discussions," Alexei said.

"I did, but we don't need suits."

Alexei looked puzzled.

"Why not?"

"Because Roscoe, our driver, brought these."

Julius opened the closet. Several full-length robes hung there.

"According to Malcolm, every participant must wear one!"

Alexei and Julius entered the main hallway ten minutes early. The plain dark gray robes were big enough for Alexei to wear slacks and a button-down shirt underneath it. He left the tie and sports coat behind.

"You're early. Excellent!" Malcolm said. "The other guests have arrived."

Malcolm led them to an adjacent room. Several tables had various food and beverages. Alexei recognized Hunter, but he didn't know who the other man was.

"Let me introduce our guests," Malcolm said. "From The Collective, we have Alexei Breven and Julius Shcherbakov."

Alexei raised his glass in a toasting motion.

"From Black Iris, Hunter Garrison and Jony Clarke."

Hunter nodded. Jony was expressionless, like a statue.

The men sized up their competition.

"I want to propose a toast to a productive and satisfactory dialogue," Alexei said.

Hunter and Jony raised their glasses, but the motion

seemed devoid of any meaning. Alexei thought he could hear the crackle of energy in the room. Having sensed the tension, Malcolm steered the men into the dining hall, where a three-course meal was served. Alexei noticed that Hunter had a visible limp.

Alexei was tired of Hunter's brooding and tried to lighten the mood by engaging in some polite conversation. "What do you think of this facility? Magnificent, isn't it?" Alexei said to Hunter.

"I would expect nothing less from the Shadow Dealers," Hunter replied.

"Since dinner is over, shall we take our places at the table?" Malcolm asked.

Everyone followed Malcolm into the main negotiating hall.

"It is beautiful," Alexei said.

"What is?" Hunter asked.

"The sunset. I find that you gain perspective by taking time to appreciate the beauty around us."

Hunter said something under his breath.

Everyone was greeted by a young woman.

"I'm Melissa. I will be documenting the proceedings."

Hunter looked at Melissa for a long moment, then nodded approval. *If I didn't know better, I'd think young Hunter is smitten,* Alexei thought.

Malcolm reminded the group of the rules. Once a verbal "I agree" was issued from each participant, he said, "Let the record show that the current time is 7:31 p.m. on December 25th. The floor will be given to Black Iris for opening remarks. Remember, no interruptions. Who will represent Black Iris?"

"I speak for Black Iris," Hunter said. "On November 26th,

a bounty, placed by Gregor, an active member of The Collective, was issued and a deposit was made. On December 4th, the bounty was removed. Using my right of reactivation, I decided to collect on the bounty. That action caused a worm to awaken and infect our entire Black Iris site. Our researchers determined that the worm was related to GreyWorm, which was written by Gregor. Also, no existing traces of this variant of the worm can be found anywhere on the surface or Dark Web, which means it is unique enough that no one but Gregor or The Collective could have it. We demand the five million Digibit that was stolen from us. Other demands include the cost of downtime to our systems and estimated member costs, which is worth over 300,000 pound sterling. Also, as a gesture of good faith, we demand the services of Natasha Solikov for three weeks. That is what Black Iris demands."

Malcolm took a pause for dramatic effect, then said, "The Collective may respond."

"The evidence presented so far is circumstantial in nature, and I demand additional proof of the breach to Black Iris systems," Alexei began. "Furthermore, Gregor was burned around the time of your system breach. He had no official support from anyone from The Collective. I'm prepared to reimburse you for your actual loss of Digibit, but I require proof, such as ledger transactions from wallets, network traffic logs from the time of the breach, etc. I want restitution for my associate, who suffered directly when Hunter was carrying out the bounty on Nigel Watson." Alexei pointed at Julius's arm sling to make his point. "Nigel should not have been targeted. He is an intern that has not been completely read into the inner-workings of The Collective. He is at a disadvantage and should not be targeted. Also, Natasha will not work for anyone but me. You may ask her directly, but I can assure you the answer will be no."

"I suggest we take a small break before continuing. Private break rooms are available for members of each group," Malcolm said.

Hunter glared at Alexei before getting up and motioning Jony to follow.

Alexei motioned for Julius to join him in the other break room.

"What do you know about Hunter?" Alexei asked.

"I know he is deadly. Rumor has it he received extensive ninja-like training since he was a child. He also has a temper."

"And his rank in Black Iris?"

"Word on the street is he's related to the founder."

"Dahlia? The Black Heart herself!"Alexei shivered at the memory of Black Heart.

"Have you ever had any run-ins with Black Heart?" Julius asked.

"I met her about twenty years ago. I had just ended my mandatory two-year service with the military. We worked for the same person, a ruthless man named Sarrin. We were an item. I ended it because her appetite for blood was more important to her than I was."

Julius followed Alexei back to the meeting room.

"I trust that the meetings were productive?" Malcolm asked. "Are we ready to resume the dialogue?"

Both Alexei and Hunter nodded in agreement.

"Black Iris will have the opportunity to respond."

"We demand that The Collective pay what is owed. No exceptions! The damage to Julius is covered under collateral damage rules. We feel that The Collective needs to pay in full for what they did to us or we'll—"

Jony kicked Hunter under the table, and he abruptly stopped talking. He shot a murderous glance at Alexei.

No one spoke for at least a minute. Malcolm broke the silence. "Black Iris, do you have anything else to add?"

"No!" Hunter snapped.

"The Collective will now be given the opportunity to respond."

"Our counteroffer is fair and reasonable. I offered full monetary restitution for the stolen Digibit, but I need proof. Otherwise, what will stop any other organization from demanding payment for future unsubstantiated behavior? The demand for 300,000 pounds is preposterous. The Dark Web runs on Digibit, not British pounds!"

Hunter rose suddenly, his chair thrown to the floor. He slapped the table hard enough to make it shake. Alexei was close enough to notice the faint outline of a scar that ran across his left cheek, ending at his mouth.

"It's not your turn to respond. I will not tolerate another outburst!" Malcolm said.

Jony grabbed Hunter by the wrist and motioned for him to be seated.

"It is late. I suggest we conclude for the evening. I trust that cooler heads will prevail in the morrow," Malcolm said.

Alexei returned to his suite. *Why did Black Iris send this cretin to represent their interests?* He was missing something, and he didn't like the feel of the situation.

Alexei's thoughts were interrupted by a loud knock on the door. When Alexei opened the door, he was jostled by Jony, Hunter's second.

"What are you doing here?" Alexei demanded.

Jony sauntered around the room. Alexei watched the man for several seconds before Jony spoke. "Hunter is not himself tonight. He's usually a level-headed bloke. I wanted to apologize for his behavior. It is rude and unbecoming of Black Iris."

"The kid—Hunter—seems to have some bias toward me, toward The Collective," Alexei said.

"Hunter was punished for taking action on the bounty that injured your man. Coming here to parley is part of his punishment. I think he is being tested by his mum," Jony said.

"Dahlia?"

"Umm, never mind me. I said too much," Jony said as he left.

Alexei remained in deep thought for a long time. He was uneasy with the situation. The discussions had not resolved anything, only heightened tensions.

Alexei woke to a knocking sound. Malcolm was waiting for him when he answered the door to his suite.

"Sorry to bother you at such an ungodly hour, but you are needed in the meeting room."

Alexei put on a robe and trudged down to the main meeting room. Julius was waiting for him.

"Why have I been summoned at 2 a.m.?" Alexei demanded.

"I'm afraid Black Iris will not be participating in any additional dialogue," Malcolm said. "About an hour ago, we received an urgent communiqué. There has been a simultaneous cyber and physical attack against Black Iris. There is evidence of The Collective's involvement."

Alexei couldn't believe it.

"In light of this news, I suggest that you return," Malcolm said.

"It wasn't us!"

"The Shadow Dealers are not here to pass judgment. We are a neutral party. We have taken the liberty of collecting your belongings. We will now transport you and your associate back to the mainland."

Nigel pressed the button to summon the nurse. He was out of ice chips. His throat felt so raw, he could barely swallow, and he couldn't talk. Sleep was coming in spurts. When it did, he saw this face—intense green eyes and a scar that ran across this face. The worst part was the intense hatred that this guy's expression revealed. One of the most disturbing things was that the guy was young, older than Nigel but not by much. Three years maximum! Nigel shuttered at the thought.

Nurse Sandy appeared with a new IV, a bag of ice chips, and a fresh spoon. The room looked different, too. The previous room had an empty bed next to his; this was a private room. *Have they switched rooms on me?*

"Merry Christmas, Nigel."

Was it Christmas already?

"Oh, I almost forgot. You have a visitor."

Nigel started writing. He presented the nurse with a note that read, "Who?"

"A couple of girls."

The nurse exited the room and escorted two teenagers in. Nigel's heart seemed to miss a beat when he saw Jet. He recognized the second girl as Cassidy, who had been instrumental in facilitating a video chat that seemed to raise more questions than it answered. He gave Jet as large of a smile as his stitches allowed. Jet smiled but could not hold it as tears started to flow. She was at a loss for words. She held Nigel's hand for a long time.

"How you feeling, Nigel?" Cassidy said.

Nigel responded by writing on his notepad.

"Can't speak. Hurts like hell. Can swallow drops of water from the ice chips."

Cassidy read the note, then showed Jet. Nigel wrote for a long time before giving the pad of paper back to Cassidy. He briefly recounted the events of the past several days.

"When can you go home?"

"Soon, I hope," Nigel wrote.

Cassidy felt the buzzing of her phone. "I need to take this." She stepped outside.

"Please don't talk, my love," Jet said.

Nigel felt his face flush.

"My father doesn't understand the bond that we both share. We have been through a lot in a short time. Our connection runs deep. When I was in the hospital, he found a new place for us to live. I had to move just after coming home. He doesn't know that I'm here."

"Where do you live now?"

"Newport, almost a two-hour drive. My dad thinks I'm visiting Cassidy."

Jet paused to collect her thoughts. Nigel resumed his scribbling, ripped out a page, then handed Jet the note, which read, "How long are you here for?"

"I need to start driving back after my visit."

Nigel's mouth trembled. He was filled with emotion that he never felt before.

"I can stay for a while."

Nigel held Jet's hand for a long time.

"Nigel?"

Nigel and Jet turned to see Ellen and Ralphie sanding in the doorway. Nigel didn't know how long they had been there.

He lost track of time. Nigel waved. Ralphie waved back. Milo poked his head out from behind Ellen.

"Who is this?" Ellen asked.

"Her name is Jet," Milo said.

Jet extended a hand, and Ellen shook it. She gave Nigel a nod.

"The doctor said you can come home later today. He will be in soon to check your stitches and to go over your at-home healing plan."

Nigel grinned. This was the best news he had all week.

"I need to drive back to Newport before dark. I will text you or see you online, Nige."

Nigel blew her a kiss, and Jet's cheeks turned red as crimson as she returned the gesture. The exchange was not lost on Ellen. She was happy that Nigel had supportive friends.

"Cassidy, do you need a ride home?" Jet asked.

"Mrs. Watson can take me."

"I no longer have a car. I had to sell it to pay Nigel's attorney." Ellen looked down as she said the words.

"That's okay, Mrs. Watson. Milo and I will grab a ride share home."

Jet sneaked another glance at Nigel before beginning the long ride home.

Nigel, Ellen, and Ralphie sat around a borrowed Christmas tree. Although they had few gifts, they were thankful that everyone was free. Nigel's throat was still bandaged, but in time, it should make a full recovery.

"How about a game?" Ralphie asked.

"What do you have in mind?" Nigel replied.

"Slides and Ladders?"

"Set it up," Nigel said.

Ellen was pleased that her boys enjoyed playing together, especially after the recent events. For the first time in a long while, she felt at peace. The community had been supportive as well. Mr. Henry gave them the tree; other neighbors provided meals.

The doorbell rang.

"Merry Christmas, Agent Appleton," Ellen said.

"Is this a good time? I don't want to intrude."

"It's cold out. Please, come inside."

Ellen took John's coat and hung it in the closet.

"What brings you to Milford?"

"I feel that I owe you and your family an apology. I made several terrible mistakes."

"Why the change of heart?" Ellen asked.

"Nigel opened my eyes in the hospital. I was so focused on a bust, I failed to see all the facts. I was blinded by my bias. Nigel was instrumental in helping me piece together what really happened. After revisiting the evidence, I saw the real truth: Nigel was being set up. The worst part about it was that I inadvertently spoiled some of the evidence. The hacker we caught was let go. Friends at the FBI helped me track down other evidence as well. As it turns out, the hacker group that Gregor led was responsible for your hack as well."

Ellen felt a rush of emotions. She wanted to claw Agent Appleton's eyes out, but she controlled her breathing and calmed down. She didn't want to ruin the day by losing her temper. It was Christmas, and her family was together.

"You don't know how hard it is to say this, but I forgive you, Agent Appleton."

John looked astonished. He hadn't expected that at all. It made what he was about to do next that much more gratifying. He reached into his pocket and pulled out a ring box.

Ellen gasped. "What is this?"

John opened the ring box. A small key against blue velvet was visible. He also handed her a piece of paper which he had signed.

"This is the key to your new car," John said as he handed her the rest of the car keys. "I know you had to sell your car to pay your legal fees, so this is the least I can do. The car is nothing fancy, but please use it in good health."

Ellen was stunned. She couldn't think of anything else to say. She could feel the tears roll down her face.

"Thank you, John, and God bless you."

John was startled as Ellen gave him a bear hug. "Will you stay for dinner? I was just about to take it out of the oven."

John nodded, then followed Ellen to the dining room.

"Boys, we have a dinner guest!"

ABOUT THE AUTHOR

D. B. Goodin has a passion for writing since grade school. After publishing several non-fiction books, Mr. Goodin ventured into the craft of fiction to teach Cybersecurity concepts in a less intimidating fashion. Mr. Goodin works as a Principal Cybersecurity Analyst for a major software company based in Silicon Valley and holds a Masters in Digital Forensic Science from Champlain College.

Made in the
USA
Columbia, SC